Darby held out her hand, hoping the filly would sniff it.

The sorrel's head lashed out like a striking snake's.

Darby jerked her hand back and sidestepped at the same time.

She doesn't want to be touched, that's for sure, Darby thought, but the filly's feint had been so far off target, Darby hadn't even felt a puff of air at the movement. Hoku hadn't meant to bite her—just warn her that things were different now.

The filly shifted restlessly, waiting to see what Darby did next.

"She was just threatening, wasn't she?" Darby muttered without looking away. She had to be sure.

"This time," her grandfather answered.

Check out the
Phantom Stallion
series, also by Terri Farley!

Phantom Stallion

WILD HORSE ISLAND 1

THE HORSE CHARMER
TERRI FARLEY

HarperTrophy®
An Imprint of HarperCollins*Publishers*

Acknowledgments

The spirit of Aloha was extended to me by many people, including Linda Lindsay, Dennise and Sonny Stires, Laura Thompson, Dr. Billy Bergin, Gail Fujimoto, and the Dahana Ranch cowboys—Tyler, Kai, Kaulana, and especially B.J. On the mainland, my thanks go to my insightful agent Karen Solem, the HarperCollins crew, and family and friends. Even when I drive you crazy, you rarely let it show. That means I'm ready to jump in and do it again!

Disclaimer

Wild Horse Island is imaginary. Its history, culture, legends, people, and ecology echo Hawaii's, but my stories and reality are like leaves on the rain forest floor. They may overlap, but their edges never really match.

The Horse Charmer

Library of Congress Catalog Card Number: 2006937686
ISBN-10: 0-06-081542-6 — ISBN-13: 978-0-06-081542-4

Typography by Jennifer Heuer
❖
First Harper Trophy edition, 2007

This book is dedicated to Kylie Ka'eo and Mervina Cash-Ka'eo, who welcomed me to Hawaii with warmth, flowers, and incredible willingness to teach me all things Hawaiian. . . .

And to the Nakoa family—Harry, Kiyo, Ku'uipo, Dustin, Ikena, and Pa'akaula—of the Big Island's Dahana Ranch. They took me to magical places, joined in my author's what-if-ing, and fulfilled childhood dreams of living in a world of horses.

Mahalo Nui Loa!

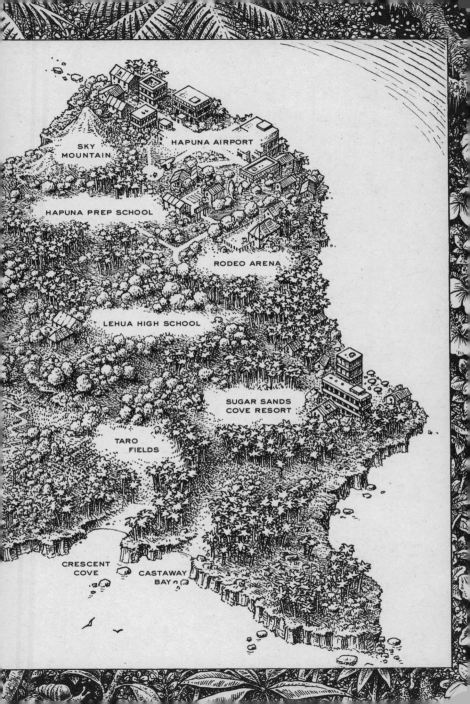

SKY
MOUNTAIN

HAPUNA AIRPORT

HAPUNA PREP SCHOOL

RODEO ARENA

LEHUA HIGH SCHOOL

SUGAR SANDS
COVE RESORT

TARO
FIELDS

CRESCENT
COVE

CASTAWAY
BAY

1

THE HORSE CHARMER

Chapter 1

In the dream, horses trot alongside her through a jungle. Burnished bay, black, roan, and glimmering gray, they canter under vines that trail over them, leaving their tails strewn with scarlet flowers. Their nostrils flare to smell the honey-sweet air. Their hooves thump a wild rhythm while rain patters on overhead leaves that wave like green elephant ears.

Darby follows a red dirt path, though she doesn't know where it leads. Even when the trail slopes down, ever steeper, and the rain's hiss crowds into her ears, she isn't afraid. The horses press close all around her.

She is one of them, until the rain stops.

The horses halt.

With undersea slowness, Darby turns to ask them why. Heads tossing, manes slapping their necks, the horses' uneasy milling tells her they can't go on.

She pivots in a shaft of sunlight. Brightness slanting through the treetops spotlights a clearing. It wasn't there a minute ago. Neither was the dollhouse-small shack.

Rain drips from its metal roof. Rust streaks its walls. A white curtain billows out a window and strange music coaxes Darby to walk closer.

The horses watch as Darby's bare feet take her right up to the wooden door.

Slowly, inch by inch, it is creaking open. . . .

"Honey, you really didn't have time for a nap."

Darby Carter's eyes snapped open.

Car keys jingled. Her mom stood next to the couch, smiling down at her. "Your last day at school tired you out."

"I guess," Darby managed, but then her confusion lifted.

Her last day of school—at least for a few weeks— had come early; it was still only March.

She shook her head, stared at the suitcases and backpack waiting next to the front door, and realized she wasn't in a jungle.

She was in her apartment, but struggling out of the dream was like pushing aside those tropical vines she'd imagined. At last she sat up and her eyes wandered to the television. The five o'clock news was coming on.

Panic zinged her nerves. "We're supposed to leave at five!"

"Yep, let's go," her mom said.

Suitcases stowed, doors slammed, and seat belts cinched, they sped down the block, dared a yellow light to take their freeway entrance, and headed toward the Los Angeles International Airport.

"You can still change your mind," her mom said. Hands gripping the car's steering wheel, Ellen Carter glanced sideways at her daughter. "I can turn around," she added, and when Darby didn't respond, her voice turned serious. "Right this minute."

"It's okay, Mom. I want to go," Darby said.

After all, why should she feel homesick? It wasn't like she'd miss the smog, noise, and sirens. Or school.

She and her mom didn't live in the best neighborhood. Darby's middle school was known for rough hallway encounters and a vice principal who thought a rigid dress code could cure just about any problems the students had.

Darby had a different strategy. She'd learned that scuttling down the halls with her eyes lowered made her look like a loser and attracted the wrong kind of attention. So she always walked as tall as a five-foot eighth grader could, and pretended to search the tide of faces for her best friend Heather, even when she knew Heather had class on the other side of campus.

That worked pretty well unless an asthma attack forced Darby into a bathroom to use her inhaler. There, she faced waves of cigarette smoke—which only made it harder to breathe—or the accusing stares of girls writing lipstick graffiti on the mirrors.

She got the same looks from the kids in class, when teachers required her to answer questions.

She wouldn't, *couldn't*, fake being dumb. Neither could Heather, and that's how they'd ended up friends. Most days they'd split a sandwich between class and the library, then spend their lunchtimes reading. After school they'd e-mail back and forth and talk on the phone about horses.

Darby sighed.

"Do you have all your medicine? What about your ticket?"

"No, Mom, I threw them out the window," Darby joked, but her mother didn't seem to notice. When her mother leaned forward to squint through the windshield, Darby felt a jab of guilt and checked her backpack pocket for her plane ticket.

Her mother couldn't afford to get the new contact lenses she needed, but she'd found the money for the flight that would take Darby across the ocean.

Mom, Darby thought, *I'm really going to miss you.* But she didn't say it, and then she couldn't, because brake lights glared in front of them like a thousand red eyes.

Her mother sucked in a breath and made a worried sound before she muttered, "We'll make it."

"You can drop me off in front," Darby said.

She'd just turned thirteen. She could make her way through the terminal and figure out where she was going, right?

Still, Darby crossed her fingers, hoping her mom wouldn't take her up on the offer.

"Of course I can't," her mother said, but she didn't sound firm about it. Suddenly she yelled at a driver weaving in front of them, "Hey! Would it kill you to hang up and drive?"

As soon as she'd finished yelling, they laughed. She and Darby both knew that if her mom's cell phone rang and the number displayed was her agent's, nothing, including L.A.'s next big earthquake, would keep her from answering.

Darby's mother, Ellen Carter, was an actress, and she'd been awaiting her big break for as long as Darby could remember. Darby didn't try to fool herself. She knew part of the reason her mom was letting her ugly duckling daughter go off without her for six months was so she could concentrate on her career.

Ellen Carter claimed that when she'd been married to Darby's father, she'd been happy staying with Darby in an apartment above a pizza parlor, but Darby couldn't picture it. And she knew her parents had broken up over her mom's love of acting.

Long black hair swooped around her mom's amber skin, framing her exotic eyes. In fact, "exotic and ethnic" was the niche her mom filled for casting directors, though she'd never played a Hawaiian character, which was sort of ironic, because Hawaiian was what she was. At least half.

And that made Darby one-quarter Hawaiian, which no one would have guessed from her stick-straight black hair and blue eyes. Her heritage would never have been a big deal except that that's where she was headed now. To Hawaii. Not the touristy, white sand beach and big hotel part, either. She was going to the real Hawaii, where her mom had grown up.

Just because Mom swore never to go back there, doesn't mean I won't like it, Darby told herself. So what if her mother—with the exception of a single phone call— had kept her fifteen-year promise never to speak to her Hawaiian father again?

Darby swallowed hard. She was still mad at her mom for hiding half her family from her for her entire life.

Like a freeze-frame in a movie, Darby saw herself sitting in the barn on Deerpath Ranch in Nevada, watching as a beautiful filly kicked and cried, emerging from the sedated sleep that had made it possible for her to be transported from the Nevada range to a barn.

Darby's eyes had followed the gleam of lantern light on the mustang's red-gold coat and tawny mane, as her mom confessed, "Your grandfather isn't dead.

You have a great-aunt and a great-grandmother, too, in Hawaii."

Her mother had explained that Darby's grandfather was a paniolo, one of a long line of Hawaiian cowboys who'd galloped beaches and volcanic slopes years before mainland cowboys.

I'm descended from paniolo, Darby had thought in amazement. *No wonder I was born with horses in my heart.*

And then, it was like fate stepped in.

Her mother's agent called to tell her she'd won a role in a movie shooting on location in Tahiti. If she accepted, she'd be gone for two months, and since Darby couldn't tag along or stay alone in their apartment, her mom had given her a choice.

"You can stay with your dad," she had said. "Or, if you want to meet your grandfather—for you, I'll call him."

Even as she'd watched her mom's mouth form the words, Darby had known this decision would shape her life. She'd stay on a safe, familiar track if she lived with her father and his second family in the same above-the-pizza-parlor apartment he'd once shared with her mom.

She didn't think she was gutsy enough to pack her bags and move to Hawaii, to a place where her mom couldn't drive all night to reach her in an emergency.

But courage came from a weird place. Darby had fallen in love with a mustang. To keep that wild horse, she'd do anything. When her grandfather had invited her to adopt the horse and bring it along to his ranch, Darby knew that doing *anything* meant moving in with a grandfather she'd never met.

"There's our exit. Hang on," her mom said now, and then they were careening across traffic, missing the other cars by inches.

When her mom drove right past the sign pointing to the parking garage and pulled up next to a curb marked DROP OFF, Darby felt a tightening in her chest.

"You said it was okay," her mom reminded her.

"It is," Darby insisted. She tried to sound casual.

Her mother must have sensed something was wrong, though, because she ignored the robotic voice telling them this was only a loading zone. She turned off the car and reached across to place her hand on Darby's shoulder.

Darby looked down, frowning as if it took every bit of her concentration to release her seat belt. If her mom got all mushy, they'd both cry.

"You'll love the ranch. You'll be in heaven," her mom told her, but Darby didn't look up until she added, "And you'll get along with *him* just fine. You're different than I am."

Yeah, Darby thought, *you have enough nerve for two of us. Why didn't you pass any on to me?*

But she didn't say that. Instead, she asked, "What does that mean?"

"He loves horses and so do you."

Darby tried to read her mom's mind instead of her happy face. She would have believed her mom if only she hadn't found that crumpled letter in the trash.

"What if loving horses isn't enough?" Darby whispered.

"It will be," her mom assured her. "Horses have given you a new sense of . . ." She looked up for a minute, as if searching for the perfect word. "Determination."

"I don't know."

"What about that horse camp? You bullied me into letting you go off to Nevada—"

"I've never bullied you," Darby insisted.

"—Then you saved that horse—"

"You keep saying that! I didn't save her."

"All I know is, when I got there, I saw this wild mustang gazing at you with love in her eyes. I *did*. And as your grandfather will be more than happy to tell you, you sure didn't get your horse sense from—" Her mom stopped.

They sat quietly, neither wanting to be the first to open the car door and leave the other.

Then a uniformed guard rapped on the car window.

"Okay, sweetie." Darby's mom leaned forward and kissed her cheek.

As Darby climbed out of the car and closed the door, she noticed that the sidewalk was crowded with people going places. The smell of jet fuel mixed with perfume and coffee in takeout cups. Automatic doors into the terminal opened and closed, letting out party-loud noise. And suddenly, excitement replaced Darby's fear.

She could do this.

Darby patted her pockets and checked her back-pack. Her book, medicine, ticket, and the little spiral-bound notebook in which she'd write down Hawaiian words and the names of people, places, and horses were all where they should be.

She grabbed her suitcases and squared her shoulders just as her mom wrapped her in a hug. Darby clutched the suitcase handles harder. She refused to cry, but she couldn't help one little gulp.

Her mom stepped back, lifted Darby's chin, and flashed her movie-star smile.

"I'm not worried about you, baby, and do you know why?"

Suddenly her mom's movie-star smile was replaced with a genuine grin. "Because my daughter could never be unhappy in a place called Wild Horse Island!"

Darby lunged forward for a final, breathless hug, and hoped her mother was right.

The flight across the Pacific Ocean went on for-ever.

It was only after she'd changed planes for the last

leg of her journey that Darby unfolded the stiff, moss-green paper she was using as a bookmark and tried once more to smooth out its wrinkles. Yawning, she read the letter one more time.

> *Dear Daughter,*
> *You, Darby, and her horse are welcome here, and I am grateful for the chance to teach her of her family, her ʻaumakua, and horses. You say she is timid, but the picture of her with the* pueo*-marked horse shows me sleeping bravery. You must remember that it is the grandparents' right to take as* hanai *the* hiapo, *but we will let Darby herself decide.*
>
> > *Sincerely,*
> > *Jonah*

It didn't make any more sense now than it had when she'd found it just a few hours ago. Did her mom speak Hawaiian? Considering how Darby had found the discarded note, she didn't have the nerve to ask. And when she'd tried to look the words up on the Internet, Mom had spotted her, thrown her hands up in frustration, and insisted Darby did not have time to be fooling around on the computer.

The letter held no clues to what the Hawaiian words meant.

Her grandfather's declaration that he saw her "sleeping bravery" was the most confusing part of all.

The bravest thing she'd ever done was lie down next to the wild filly in Nevada. But she'd been shaking as she lowered herself into the snow that day.

The sensible part of Darby's brain said she'd just been lucky that the stunned mustang had accepted her. If the filly had tried to bite or strike out with her forelegs, Darby would have scurried out of reach and waited for help.

No, you would not.

Darby settled back in her seat, smiling, and her eyes closed. Then she was back in the dream.

She could smell wet earth and warm horses. Flat green leaves were tambourines for a rainstorm and droplets sparkled on black horse tails just out of reach. Huffing grassy breath, the horse on her left snorted a question. A horse on her right rubbed shoulder to shoulder with Darby as they trotted. Hooves thudded and thumped behind her, but her bare toes were safe. Every mare, foal, and stallion made room for her. She was part of the herd.

Until the horses stopped.

Exposed and alone, Darby didn't want to go on without them, but she had no choice. Her feet continued along the trail. They were walking, jogging, taking her to the shabby little house. Even though she didn't know what was on the other side of the door, she was holding her breath as it creaked open and she could see . . .

The jet's wheels slammed down onto the runway

and Darby jerked awake.

Twice she'd had that same dream. *Twice.* What did that mean?

Darby tugged at the backpack she'd stuffed under the seat in front of her. She wanted to be the first one off the plane.

She couldn't waste a minute standing around. Not today, when her horse was waiting for her.

Was the mustang still confused by the truck ride from Nevada to the coast, or terrified by the week spent in a stall on a container ship? About now, the filly should be coming ashore. Would her ears prick up as she tried to make sense of the sounds of metal clanging and the ship's bottom grating on sand? Would she smell strange plants beyond the heavy scents of oil and saltwater?

For the wild filly, this was a whole new world. And Darby knew she was the only one who could make it feel like home.

Chapter 2

Music played inside the Hapuna Airport. Darby listened hard between her footfalls, but she still didn't understand the lyrics, which sounded Hawaiian. She wasn't sure what sort of instrument strummed along, either. Maybe a ukulele.

It was only six o'clock in the morning. At least, she was pretty sure it was six. Even time had changed, rolling the clock's hands back as she flew across the ocean.

Darby's eyes scanned the faces of people here to greet their friends and relatives. She watched for her grandfather. Her mom hadn't had a current photo of him, but Darby had found one that was only a year old on the Internet. He'd been standing next to a dappled-gray Quarter Horse. He had black hair and dark skin and now Darby wondered why she thought that description would be helpful. About half the people around her fit it.

She patted her pockets and mentally sorted through her backpack for the hundredth time. She had her medicine, her book with the letter wedged firmly inside, and her ticket. All at once she realized she didn't have to worry about that last one for much longer. As soon as she claimed her baggage, it would be worthless. She and her mom had decided they could only afford a one-way ticket. For now.

Darby kept walking. Everyone was smiling, but no one tried to catch her eye.

Maybe her grandfather wouldn't come alone. He might bring that cowboy, Kit—what was his last name? Darby's mind darted back to Nevada and Samantha Forster, the girl who'd introduced her to wild horses.

Thank you, thank you, thank you, Darby's brain sang silently. If she'd never met Samantha, never heard of the Dream Catcher Wild Horse Camp, never shivered on an icy highway, looking after her horse . . .

My horse. She'd waited forever to make those words real. Now, a beautiful golden filly waited for her at 'Iolani Ranch.

Ely! Suddenly Darby's mind swerved back to the question she'd asked herself. That was his name. Kit Ely of Nevada was the big brother of Samantha's friend Jake. And, through some connection Darby couldn't quite recall, Kit Ely worked on her grandfather's ranch.

Darby stopped to adjust the straps of her backpack. She lifted her eyelashes just enough to confirm what she'd been afraid of. Everyone who'd gotten off her plane had been met so far, except for her.

What if no one from the ranch was coming? Could they have forgotten? She felt jittery at the idea of calling the telephone number her mom had inked into her Hawaii notebook, just in case.

But then a guy in a cowboy hat came chugging her way.

"Aloha!"

A fragrant wreath of flowers and leaves plopped over her head and settled around her neck. A burly Hawaiian guy in boots and jeans kissed her on one cheek, then the other.

Darby's mouth dropped open in surprise. She'd seen this greeting on television, but wasn't it just a hokey thing travel agencies did to welcome tourists?

She wasn't a tourist, and this guy was a real Hawaiian cowboy, built sturdy and square as a rock house.

"Hi," Darby mumbled back, too embarrassed to return his aloha.

"Darby, right?" the square cowboy asked.

"Yeah," she replied. Her cheeks blushed so hard they hurt, but his welcome warmed her. "Thank you," she added, touching the flowers.

"I'm Kimo. I work on 'Iolani Ranch." He introduced himself and sounded the syllables of the ranch name in a different way than she'd heard them in her mind.

E oh lawn ee, Darby echoed silently. It was prettier the way he said it.

"Jonah sent me for you."

She nodded as if she'd known it would be that way.

So, her grandfather hadn't come for her himself. No big deal.

"I can take that." Kimo reached for Darby's backpack.

"That's okay," she said. Imagining her pill bottles and inhaler scattering across the airport floor, she sidestepped his reach. Then added, "I have lots more, and they're heavier."

Kimo smiled as if she'd said something funny, and Darby fell into step beside him.

Picking up her suitcases took only a minute. Then Darby followed Kimo outside.

A warm breeze swirled around her. Did it pick up the fragrance of the lei around her neck, or did Hawaiian air just smell lush and flowery? The sky shone pink, blue, and silver, like the inside of a shell. Palm trees rustled and Kimo was standing by an open pickup door, waiting for her to get in.

She ducked her head, embarrassed that she'd lost

track of where they were going, but hesitated again when she noticed the painting on the truck door. A pale owl soared above turquoise letters spelling out 'IOLANI RANCH.

Kimo cleared his throat. Darby considered the long step up into the truck, then lurched up to give it a try. Once she was in, she drew a relieved breath, and even before Kimo got in to start the truck, Darby tugged her book out of her pocket and opened it.

After leaving the airport, Kimo cruised down a street of small businesses and past a building with a flagpole. He claimed it was the island's biggest town.

"Don't blink or you'll miss it," he said as they turned onto the highway.

He was trying to be nice, so Darby nodded, wishing she could chatter and make friends the way other girls did. Kimo didn't seem to mind her silence. Even though she kept her eyes on her book, he pointed out a private school, cone-shaped peaks that were actually volcanoes, and a beach front resort called Sugar Sands Cove.

Salt air rushed in the truck windows, swirling the ends of Darby's ponytail in front of her eyes. She tossed her head, thinking of her filly doing the same thing, and tried to get up the nerve to ask Kimo about her horse. How had she tolerated the long shipboard journey?

"My horse . . ." Darby began, but the sound of breaking waves and a truck engine came through the open windows and Kimo just shot her a puzzled look as if she'd made a weird noise.

"You like horses?" Kimo asked, so maybe he'd kind of heard her.

"I love horses!"

"Kit's at the harbor with Cade, waiting for your horse to come in," he said.

"My—wait," Darby said. "She's not at the ranch yet?"

"Quarantine in Honolulu," Kimo pointed out, as if that explained everything.

Quarantine?

"It's routine," he added. "All animals from the mainland have to be checked out and observed to make sure they're healthy."

"And she was?" Darby asked.

"She's arriving today, so I guess so," he said. Minutes later, as if he'd been mulling it over, he added, "You haven't met Jonah, yeah?"

Darby shook her head.

"So, you haven't met Cade."

She shook her head again. "Is he a cowboy, like you?"

"Not like me," Kimo said with a laugh Darby couldn't exactly interpret. "He's *hanai*'d to Jonah."

Kimo must have seen her seize on the word from her grandfather's letter, because he frowned while Darby tried to pull her thoughts into a logical sentence.

Hanai the *hiapo* . . . Was that what the letter had said?

"What's *hanai*?" she demanded.

"Like adoption," Kimo explained.

Ten minutes later, Darby was still wondering why a grandfather would be adopting kids, and Kimo slid open the truck's sunroof. Birdsong and the scents of wet dirt and more flowers floated in.

"You wanna go down through Crimson Vale or take the ridge road?" he asked. "One's faster. The other has wild horses. The valley's full of waterfalls, ponds covered with lily pads, and . . ." He gazed out the windshield, skyward. "Days like this, rainbows."

"That's a terrible choice to have to make," she accused, but when Kimo quit laughing, Darby had already decided. "The fast one. I have to be there when my horse arrives."

"We'll chance 'em," Kimo said.

He leaned forward and began speeding around swooping turns. The switchbacks came so close together, Darby couldn't brace for them, and she realized the cowboy had taken her words as a dare.

She should have warned him she was prone to car sickness, but it was too embarrassing.

The pineapple juice she'd had hours ago on the plane turned sour in her stomach. And then her throat.

"I've got to stop," she said, trying not to whine.

"You picked a good place," Kimo said. "Nice

view. Just watch your step. There's a—"

Darby was out of the truck and across the road before he could finish. Her stomach rolled and heaved. She felt awful.

She glanced back to see Kimo watching, and kept walking. She meandered along a faint path and her head pounded.

Aloha, welcome to your new home.

Thanks so much, but I have to vomit.

The trees crowded closer to her. Shaded by a tunnel of morning glory vines, she felt a little better. Trumpet-shaped flowers hung upside down, tissue thin and paper white.

Coming out of the fragrant tunnel, she saw two slabs of black rock, fallen against each other like a teeter-totter. A landmark, she thought. Passing that would take her back to the road.

Okay, she'd be fine, but she needed to walk a little longer, just to be sure.

A nice view, Kimo had said, and all at once, dead ahead, she saw nothing but air and sky. Her feet stopped, but the skidding of her shoes sent pebbles plummeting over the edge of a cliff.

Didn't Hawaiians believe in protecting people from their own stupidity?

A drop-off. That's what Kimo had shouted after her. Darby's mind swam, trying to estimate how far she would have fallen. A mile? Two?

Her next step would have taken her off the edge,

past the face of the sea cliffs, through a circling flock of birds, down to a tiny white crescent of beach, a black finger of land, then a swath of more beach.

She felt dizzy, watching sun diamonds glinting on teal-blue waves. Dizzier as she leaned forward to see a wildlife trail twisting over the edge. . . .

Vertigo, she thought, forcing her steps back.

Something snorted.

Darby's hands jerked out to her sides for balance. She knew she couldn't have heard what she thought she had.

"You okay?" Kimo called, but Darby didn't answer.

She was listening, moving as fast as her hammering heart would allow, and hoping the snorter wasn't anything dangerous, when she glimpsed movement through a narrow gap in the trailside foliage.

There, she saw a horse's black face. It had one brown eye and one blue eye and both of them were watching her.

Chapter 3

Darby's chest hurt, but she managed to tell Kimo she'd seen a wild horse.

"Not up here. Not unless you saw a spirit horse." Kimo's voice slowed. "Some old-timers try to scare people out of the valley by saying spirits of the *ali'i* buried in the cliffs would come after them, and some had horses killed to go along with them as death companions."

Because Kimo's tone wasn't scare-the-kid creepy, but matter-of-fact like a teacher's, Darby found the nerve to interrupt him.

"Buried in the cliffs?"

"Sure." Kimo pointed toward the foliage between them and the drop-off. "There are caves overlooking the sea. In ancient times, they lowered a 'volunteer' on a rope with the body of a great leader. It was supposed to be a big honor, carrying royalty down to a final resting place, but to keep its location secret, the volunteer killed himself. There's a serious *kapu*, you know, taboo, keeping people away from those caves."

Like Egyptians and pyramids, Darby mused, but one thing she knew for sure was that the snorting horse had not been a spirit.

As they drove, she stared into the greenery flanking the road.

She searched for the black face shining like satin, and the crystal-blue eye that wasn't scary, but beautiful and surprising like a mislaid jewel.

At last, Kimo turned off the patchwork of asphalt onto a smooth dirt road that ran through acres of pastures.

At first, Darby didn't see any horses. The fields on the right side of the road weren't even fenced.

It certainly looked like a ranch, with large corrals and trailers scattered here and there. As they drove closer, Darby spotted a two-story house. Would that—or maybe one of the two cottages she saw just ahead—be her new home?

"Welcome to 'Iolani Ranch," Kimo said.

Straight ahead, a pale-green house sat beside a matching shed. As Darby studied them, she had the weirdest feeling that the paddock that was set into the knoll's curve on her right, and the house perched on the bluff to her left, formed arms, reaching out to hug her.

Lose the overactive imagination, Darby told herself, but she was smiling as Kimo pulled up next to a battered brown Land Rover in front of the house.

Past the house, she got a quick glimpse of hills sprinkled with horses, a band of dark trees, twin volcanoes, and Sky Mountain, before a neigh made her turn.

Yes! At last!

Trotting across one of the unfenced fields came a little band of horses. Two grays, a bay, and, a few steps ahead of the others, a huge black horse with rust-brown rings around his eyes.

He moved with the heavy grace of a knight's charger. He grabbed mouthfuls of grass as he came, but he was definitely headed their way.

"Is he yours?" Darby asked Kimo, but she was already climbing out of the truck. The cowboy shook his head and grabbed his hat.

"Aloha, welcome!" A woman her mom's age burst out of the house. For a second Darby thought she was about to get another cheek-kissing greeting, but the woman just brushed her messy, dark-blond bob behind her ears and beamed at Darby.

"Hi," Darby said cautiously. Should she recognize this woman who looked so glad to see her?

"I'm Cathy Kato, ranch manager, bookkeeper—"

"Cook," Kimo put in.

Cathy made a wavering motion with one hand. "He's being kind. My meals are nothing special. Pretty much catch-as-catch-can."

"I'm used to that," Darby said with a smile.

"I've got breakfast ready when you are," Cathy said. "And we'll put your things in the room at the end of the hall. If you need anything, Megan and I live just upstairs. Megan's a sophomore at Lehua High. And you'll be a freshman, is that right?"

"Yes," Darby said, but Cathy's words had come at her so fast, she felt dazed, then thought, *But not until next year.*

Then, as if she couldn't help herself, Cathy reached out and gave Darby's hand a squeeze. "I'm so glad you're here."

Darby was about to ask *why* when a bunch of dogs burst over a hill behind the horses.

"Jonah's pack," Cathy said, then added something about getting back to work, but Darby was distracted by the dogs.

Were they chasing the horses?

No, even she could see the horses' shying and head-tossing was high-spirited play, and not alarm at the dogs running around them.

Although she'd never had a dog, Darby thought these were a herding breed. Black, brown, and open-mouthed with excitement, they came rollicking in her direction.

There were four—no, five. The fifth was not only

smaller than the others, it was fluffy white. Its yaps were clearly intended to scare her and Kimo back into the truck.

"Simmer down, Pipsqueak," Kimo said.

Pipsqueak was a cute little dog, but the horses held Darby's attention. Ears pricked forward, eyes wide and interested, the grays and bay stopped to watch the dogs give Darby's shoes and jeans a serious sniffing.

Unconcerned, the black horse with rust-brown rings around his eyes and muzzle waded through the pack. Close up, Darby saw that he wasn't black, but midnight brown. His coat rippled over muscles that made Darby guess he was a Quarter Horse, and his eyes shone with such intelligence, Darby almost expected him to speak.

"Aren't horses supposed to be hard to catch?" Darby asked, thinking about the strategies she'd read on hiding a rope behind your leg or swishing a grain bucket.

"Sometimes," Kimo said.

"Not these guys." Darby didn't move, just let her voice coax them closer. "Not all these pretty horses."

I'm in heaven, Darby thought. The horses surrounded her, bumping soft noses at her elbows, nibbling her ponytail, and lipping the lei around her neck. She breathed in the grass and leather sweetness of them, then held out her hand toward the dark-brown horse.

"Aren't you the friendliest horses in the world? I don't have a single thing for you to eat, but you came straight to me."

Darby's arms were reaching up to hug the dark horse when a warning stopped her.

"Hey! Don't touch those horses."

Darby snatched her hand back.

The brown horse stamped impatiently, then blew through rust-shaded lips. He wasn't unsettled by the shout, but the dogs whirled to watch the man striding toward them.

If she'd seen him in downtown Los Angeles, Darby would have crossed to the other side of the street. He wasn't particularly tall and his black hair was graying at the temples, but his athletic movements had something—dignity? power? ruthlessness?—that told her he was the boss.

As if to confirm it, Kimo came up behind her and muttered, "One thing to remember about Jonah, he don't admire cowards."

So this was Jonah Kaniela Kealoha, her grandfather.

A shiver began working outward from Darby's insides. Her fingertips turned cold and her hands shook.

Her mom had never pulled cruel jokes before, so she must have forgotten that her father was terrifying.

The ground wasn't really trembling beneath his strides, Darby thought, but her mind began replaying the few times her mom had slipped up and described the real Jonah.

"After Mom died, horses were his world. . . . I was only important for the chores I could do. . . . I wasn't allowed to stay at school for play rehearsals, or go off-island for college. . . ."

Darby had overlooked those stray words, dreaming of how he'd help her tame her filly. She'd even imagined a gruff kind voice welcoming her.

Don't touch those horses.

Was it possible he hadn't recognized her?

Yeah, that was it. He must've been picturing her mom at thirteen.

What a disappointment.

Darby knew how she looked. With blue eyes too big for her face and a wide mouth that looked too soft for it, she just missed looking wimpy because of her thick, arched eyebrows. Her scrawny wrists and ankles and a back bowed from trying to catch her breath meant she certainly wasn't beautiful like her mom. The best she could hope for was that her grandfather would think she looked intelligent.

She couldn't read his mind, but that didn't seem to be the direction his thoughts had taken.

No, he'd looked her over from droopy black ponytail and pockets bulging with medicine and books, and stopped at her untied tennis shoe.

Okay, he's not impressed with me, Darby thought. *I can live with that.*

He was still the man who'd made $2,000 worth of shipping arrangements to bring her horse to Hawaii, and Darby tried to like him for that.

"Grandfather, I'm Darby." She held out her hand to him and noticed it was still shaky. "Thanks for everything."

A smile crinkled the corners of his brown eyes and lifted the hard lines around his mouth.

"You bet," he said.

Darby's heart bounced like a rubber ball when he shook her hand and she felt the hard calluses he'd earned from decades of working with horses.

"Call me Jonah," her grandfather added as he released her hand.

"Okay," Darby said. *But where's my horse?* she wanted to ask, to demand an answer, really, but she didn't want him to know she was obsessed.

Still, Jonah seemed to read her mind. "Your horse should be here any minute."

"Good," Darby said, then bit her lip to keep from asking *exactly* when.

She glanced over to see that Kimo had unloaded all her luggage. He carried it toward the house as if it didn't weigh a thing. She meant to show what great manners she had by swooping over to grab a suitcase from him, but then she saw something that made her gasp.

"It's named Sun House," her grandfather said, but it wasn't the wooden structure cantilevered over the bluff that had stunned her.

Darby's eyes had veered to the vista below the house, below the ranch yard where she stood. There was almost too much green, too many hundreds of acres of emerald pastureland for her city eyes to take in. Amid all that green, there was a world of horses.

Grazing horses, dozing horses, glossy mares with tiny, long-legged foals, horses galloping with wind-blown manes and tails, racing just because they were young and it was spring. So many horses.

Darby covered her mouth with her hands at the beauty of it. She was half afraid she'd burst out laughing.

She forced her hands back to her side and sized up the dozens of footpaths and horse trails that snaked down from where she stood to the pastures below.

The sea cliffs had been scary, but this gradual descent wasn't. It was a temptation. She imagined following her filly down there, thought of sitting on velvety grass, watching the mustang fit in with her new herd.

I could go down there, she thought, and her grandfather read her mind.

"Go ahead. Check 'em out." He sounded proud of his ranch and pleased that she appreciated it. "Kimo, go take her things on in. You can saddle Navigator, since he picked you."

The big cowboy started away and Darby looked

around to make sure her grandfather had addressed the last part of his sentence to her.

"I can't," she said. She tried to look him in the eye, but her gaze only climbed as far as his sinister black mustache.

"Can't or won't?"

Darby swallowed hard. *"Can't."*

"Speak up," he told her.

"I don't know how to saddle a horse. I've never ridden before."

She hadn't meant for the words to sound like a confession, and she couldn't tell if his expression was one of disgust or pity.

"Saddle Navigator for her," her grandfather called after Kimo.

Had he totally missed the other half of what she'd said? The "I've never ridden" part?

Kimo left her bags at the front door and turned to do as Grandfather—no, *Jonah*—asked.

One thing to remember about Jonah, he don't admire cowards.

Darby stared down the dirt road, wishing she could see her horse arriving, but she saw nothing. She didn't hear the rattle of a horse trailer or even the whoosh of far-away traffic.

Rescue wasn't coming, and Jonah was watching her, judging her. Her first hour on the ranch might set his opinion forever. She had to show him she respected him. *And* prove she wasn't a pushover.

To do both at once, she must figure out one thing: Was it braver to refuse to get on Navigator, or to swing into the saddle smiling, and show Jonah that she'd been born to ride?

 Chapter 4

"What's it gonna be?" Jonah asked.

His black eyebrows formed almost a solid line across his forehead, but he wasn't frowning. In fact, there was no hint of feeling in his tone. He looked like a man with a concealed weapon, Darby thought.

"I'll ride down there," Darby heard herself say, but her next thought was, *This had better be a dream*.

Jonah nodded, and Darby tried to match his steps. They'd almost reached a small building when he cleared his throat and said, "I don't like you to pet the horses unless they're working for you."

"Sort of like a reward?" Darby asked.

"More like recognition," Jonah answered.

Darby had always figured boundless praise and

affection opened animals' hearts, but she was surrounded by evidence that she was wrong.

The horses wandering around the ranch yard didn't act as if they'd been roped and dragged up from the pastures. They wanted to be around people, even if it meant they might have to work.

Now, for instance, as Kimo stepped out of what looked like a tack room, holding a halter, Navigator stepped forward onto the concrete area in front of the building.

What a good boy, Darby thought. Her one hand reached instinctively to stroke the horse before she pulled it back.

Wordlessly, Kimo slung the loose end of the halter rope around the gelding's neck and led him up to a ring on the outside of the tack-shed wall.

"He doesn't need petting," Jonah said. "Would your teacher pet you just for walking into class?"

"Of course not," Darby said.

"Right. These horses are my business partners. I don't want Navigator or Kona"—he pointed the horses out—"or any of them to curl up on my bed. I want a horse that respects me as I respect him, a horse that would try to swim me to the mainland if I asked him."

Kimo gave the brown gelding a brisk brushing, then flipped a saddle blanket up on his back. Darby watched every move as if she were in training, because she had a feeling that's just what this was.

Kimo eased the blanket back, off Navigator's mane, then smoothed it out with one hand while watching the horse's ears and face.

Satisfied, Kimo went back into the tack room, then came out with a heavy Western saddle.

They're going to expect me to carry one of those? Darby thought with despair.

There was no way she could copy Kimo, lifting the burdensome saddle up above the gelding's back before settling it in place. Her arms weren't strong or long enough.

"When you're riding Navigator," Jonah went on, "and he does what you ask of him, that's when you pet him."

She nodded. Why hadn't he just said that in the first place? What had sounded just plain mean before, now made sense.

"You understand?" Jonah asked.

Kimo fastened a buckle. He fed leather straps through brass circles. He looked from the stirrups to her legs, and made adjustments.

Now that it looked like she was really going to get on the horse, it occurred to her that she should have asked some questions. Was Navigator gentle? Did he tolerate beginners, or dump them in the dirt?

Up close, the brown horse looked taller, stockier, not nearly as friendly as he—wait. *He?* The name could be given to a male or female, but there was no way in the world she would ask Jonah how she could figure out a horse's sex.

"You understand what I said?" Jonah repeated.

"Yes, about not petting him," she said quietly, "but I still don't know how to ride."

Jonah sighed through his nose.

"That makes you the only member of the entire family who hasn't ridden by—what are you, thirteen?" He shook his head, then added, "It will come naturally to you."

As clearly as if he'd said it, Darby could tell that if riding *didn't* come naturally to her, Jonah would expect her to just do her best and shut up about it.

"Maybe I should get to know him better first."

"He doesn't want an engagement. He just wants you not to hurt him while you're up there." Jonah looked down. She still hadn't tied her loose shoelace. "Do you have boots?"

"Hiking boots."

"Put 'em on."

Darby sprinted into the house, unzipped her suitcase, and yanked her boots out. She hurried to put them on. Jonah's tone said he was running out of patience. She couldn't give herself time to run out of nerve.

When he saw her returning, Jonah took Navigator's reins, backed him a few steps, then led him toward a side hill.

He flipped the knotted reins over Navigator's head and said, "Go ride."

Darby looked over her shoulder at the steep slope to the pastures below. Walking the trails on her own two feet would have been easy, but could she maneuver a giant horse down them?

"You're not afraid?" he asked.

"Not on the ground."

"You're no safer on the ground than you are on his back."

Now that's comforting, Darby thought, looking at Navigator's heavy hooves.

The gelding swung his head around to study her. His forelock was wavy. He looked sweet until he pulled against the bit in his mouth and showed her teeth like piano keys.

Mount up before Jonah tells you to.

She'd read how to do this a hundred times, and even though there was no mounting block—which all the books said short riders couldn't do without—the side hill gave her some height. She'd just fling herself at Navigator's side and hope she stuck to him long enough to clamber on.

Then she realized the gelding was facing in the wrong direction.

"Left side," Darby recited under her breath as she walked around the horse. "Hold mane and reins, put a foot in the stirrup . . ."

"Where are you going?" Jonah asked.

"To get on the other side. The right side. I mean, the *correct* side. The left."

She watched his face for approval.

Then, he said, "Correct? Who told you that, the horse?"

"No."

"Try it from where you were."

Was this a trick? She glanced at Kimo.

"It's good for the horse," Kimo told her. "Keeps him loose."

Darby tightened her ponytail. If they thought she could mount from here, she probably could. All she had to do was put the movements she'd read about into action.

She faced Navigator's gleaming shoulder. She grabbed the reins and a handful of mane.

From the corner of her eye she saw Jonah watching with crossed arms.

Get it right the first time, Darby told herself.

The stirrup was as high as her shoulder, but she was flexible. She managed to get her foot in and hopped once, twice, on her other boot.

"Push up and swing!" Kimo cheered.

Her lei flew up, blinding her with flowery sweetness as she left the ground and landed in the saddle.

She'd done it. For the first time in her life, she was riding a horse.

Suddenly, she knew equestrians' secret. She knew why the cavalry scorned foot soldiers, why Native Americans who rode with the wind in their hair looked down on those who planted seeds, why

Hawaiian cowboys called paniolo sang as they rode up mountainsides beyond the reach of outsiders.

The world was a different place when you rode a horse. You looked over people and fences and everything that made you an earthbound creature. Darby could hardly wait to gallop. It would be like flying.

And then she looked down. A long, long way down.

Kimo grinned up at her, but Jonah began giving her orders.

"Gather your reins in your left hand. They should come in the bottom of your fist and flow out the top like a fountain. Then, rest your right hand on top of the saddle horn."

"Wait," Darby said. "Isn't that like riding a bike with training wheels?"

He gave her a look that asked, *Who needed training wheels if she didn't?*, then went on, "Center yourself in the saddle. Don't lean too far forward and don't hang off the right like that. Touch the horn. You don't have to cling on like your hand's a claw, but if you're balanced it will help the horse. And sit up straight!"

Darby felt the heat of her blush. He was throwing too much at her all at once, but somehow it sank into her brain. Once she was centered, she felt it.

She looked up with raised eyebrows, expecting just a pinch of praise, but Jonah had turned. Cathy's voice was calling his name.

"Telephone!" Cathy shouted as she hurried

toward him. "It's Kit and . . ."

Kit! Darby didn't hear the rest, but her heart bucked against her breastbone. Kit had gone to get her horse. He wouldn't be calling if everything was all right.

Navigator stepped forward.

"Don't squeeze your legs," Kimo whispered, putting a hand on the rein near Navigator's mouth.

"I didn't mean to," Darby said, but her eyes were on Jonah. A button beeped as he hung up the phone.

"Your filly's not happy," Jonah said.

"What's wrong?"

He shrugged. "Truck keys are in the office. C'mon, let's get 'em, then go see."

Chapter 5

Kimo caught Darby as she slipped down from Navigator's back and then pointed her toward the office. It stood next to the house and was open on one side.

Blinking her sun-dazzled eyes, Darby saw a wall of filing cabinets and two desks. A computer was perched atop one of them, surrounded by a clutter of papers.

"Lunch," Cathy said. Flashing Darby a smile that reminded her she hadn't had breakfast, Cathy shoved a brown market sack into Jonah's hands.

Jonah peeked inside, then glanced up to say, "This is Catherine Kato."

"Cathy," she corrected him quickly. "Darby and I

have met." Cathy gave a quick nod, signaling she knew Darby couldn't wait to get out of here and see her horse.

"I run the place and she tries to run me," Jonah said.

"Someone's got to," Cathy said, and Darby realized Cathy wasn't the least bit intimidated by Jonah, even if he was her boss. "I've packed sandwiches, water, and a few cookies," Cathy told Darby. "That ought to hold you until dinner."

"Thank you," Darby said, shifting from foot to foot.

"Speaking of dinner, Jonah, I'm asking Kit and Cade to come up to the house tonight."

Darby wondered if she actually shrank at the prospect of facing a bunch of strangers for her first meal at 'Iolani Ranch, or did she just feel smaller?

"Mob scene," Jonah muttered.

"There'll be six of us. We're celebrating Darby's arrival." Cathy smiled, but there was no question that her mind was made up. And Jonah went along.

"Yeah, fine," he said, then pointed toward a brown Land Rover that had the same 'Iolani Ranch owl painted on the door and said, "Let's go."

Inside, the truck wasn't nearly as cluttered as the one Kimo had driven. Every surface was shiny and smelled of the coconut oil polish she saw in a niche between the seats.

As soon as Jonah started the car and slammed the

gear shift into reverse, she wondered why that polish wasn't spilled all over the place.

Jonah wasn't a bad driver, but he jerked from full stop to foot-on-the-floor speeding. Instant whiplash, Darby thought, but she was glad Jonah was in a hurry.

"What did Kit say was wrong?" Darby blurted as they left the ranch behind. This time Jonah gave her more of an answer, but not much.

"He and Cade can't do anything with her. Kit wants to avoid sedating her."

Jonah glanced away from the road for a second.

To see how I'm taking this, Darby thought and tried not to look as scared as she felt.

"Kit's got a lot to learn, but he's made his living with horses. I hired him thinking he'd know what they needed. He thinks this one might need you."

Darby chewed her thumbnail and frowned.

"Is Cade —?" she began.

"He's my foster son. He's fifteen, I guess, and a fair hand with horses."

"Is he an orphan?" Darby asked.

"No, but his father's a fisherman," Jonah said, as if that explained everything.

Jonah picked up the lunch sack and plopped it on her lap.

"Eat," he said, and Darby guessed that meant he didn't want to answer another question.

She took the first bite of her sandwich to make

herself stay quiet, then noticed she was starving.

"This horse got a name?" Jonah asked as Darby swallowed the last of her cookie.

"Not yet," Darby admitted.

"Things name themselves if you're patient."

Darby nodded.

"So, she's a chestnut," Jonah said. "*Red* chestnut?"

"Reddish-gold," Darby said. "They called her a sorrel and she's more golden than red, with a flaxen mane and tail."

"Flaxen yellow? Or ivory?"

"Neither one," Darby said, and then, because she'd spent so many hours daydreaming about this, the words came tumbling out. "There's this color, and I only remember seeing it one other time. Mom was in this movie where she played a bride and the dress she wore was made of stuff called candlelight satin—"

"She played a bride in a movie?" Jonah leaned closer to the steering wheel.

"Yeah." Darby could hear herself boasting. "It was called—"

"I don't watch many movies."

Like a pane of glass, silence slid between them. There wasn't another sound in the truck cab until Jonah jerked the steering wheel to avoid a pothole.

"What about," he began slowly, "a Hawaiian name?"

"I can't pronounce much except *aloha* and *hula*," Darby confessed.

"We've got a cutter named Hula Girl," Jonah said, "and I don't know that much Hawaiian, anyway."

"You don't?" Darby didn't quite believe him. After all, the big thing about 'Iolani Ranch was that it had always been owned by Hawaiians.

"When I went to school, kids got beaten for speaking Hawaiian."

"Nuh-uh," Darby said in disbelief.

"See that?" Jonah held his right hand level with her eyes, as if it was some kind of proof.

And it was.

His ring finger didn't match up with the others. It kinked between the knuckles.

"Someone broke your hand for speaking Hawaiian?"

"A teacher. Not my whole hand. Just my finger."

That's terrible, she wanted to say, or *How unfair,* but her lips just glubbed as if she were a goldfish.

Jonah made a dismissing sound. "That was the old days." He pointed as the harbor office came into view, then asked, "What's that marking on your filly's chest?"

"To me it looked like a star."

She glanced over to see that Jonah's eye-crinkling smile was back.

"Hoku," he said, then turned sharply into the harbor entrance.

What had he said? They pulled up to the gate and the tall fencing with razor wire around the top caught her attention for a second.

"That name . . . did you say," Darby attempted it, kind of wincing as she said, "Joe Coo?"

"*Ho*ku," he repeated. "It means star."

He stopped the Land Rover as a guard approached.

Hoku, Darby thought silently.

"And stars are the eyes of heaven," Jonah said. "Might be a good thing to have your ancestors looking out for you."

Darby smiled nervously at that, but she kept turning the name over in her mind. She liked it.

As she tried to see past the gate for anything that looked like a place you'd keep horses, Jonah handed the guard his driver's license.

The guard jotted something on forms attached to a clipboard, returned the license, then asked, "And the girl?"

"She's my granddaughter."

Once they pulled past the gate, Darby rolled down the truck window. A sea breeze blew in to cool her, but she was listening for a neigh.

Then she spotted something high in the air over a ship: a red-orange box that looked like a cross between a cage and a stall dangled from a crane.

The horse inside was stone-still and silent, but a

high-pitched neigh came from somewhere nearby.

"That's her!" Darby shoved the truck door open and jumped down. She looked from side to side and couldn't see where the neigh was coming from, but she recognized it instantly. "That's my horse!"

Chapter 6

"Over here," Jonah said as the horse cage was lowered toward the dock.

They'd only taken a few steps when Darby saw Kit Ely coming to meet them. Tall and brown with a horseman's walk, he was older, but looked a lot like his brother Jake.

He had the "happy wolf" grin Samantha had told her about, and a stiff arm that reminded Darby that Kit's rodeo career had ended with an accident. Even though his shirt was askew and missing a button, there was a calm about Kit Ely that made Darby glad he'd been here all day, by her horse's side.

"Darby Carter," Kit said, "if your filly's half as glad to see you as I am, our troubles are over." His hands straightened his shirt as he chuckled. "That little mustang's a handful."

Darby's body tensed. "Where is she?"

Jonah held up his hand. "Let's get Kit's story before you go charging in."

"Okay," she said, but it wasn't easy.

"Not much to tell. She's afraid to unload and head-shy. Wanted a bite out of me, and caught Cade a good one."

Of course the mustang would be scared of strange humans rushing at her! What did they expect? Darby wondered.

"She'll feel better, now that they've repaired the crane and brought in her buddy," Kit said, and Darby's first impression of Kit returned. He seemed to understand.

"Her buddy?" Darby asked.

"She shipped with another horse," Kit said, glancing down at the stapled sheets of paper in his hand. "These notes are from the vet who cleared them in Honolulu. He says the shipper sent two horses: an unnamed sorrel and a bay called Judge." Kit glanced over his shoulder as the horse cage settled with a bang.

"I know Judge," Darby said, recognizing the horse. Shyness returned when she saw Jonah and Kit watching, waiting for her to go on.

"Trip didn't bother him much," Kit said, nodding at the wisp of hay Judge lipped off his shoulder, then chewed.

"Judge is the calmest horse on Mrs. Allen's ranch. You know her," she said to Kit, hoping he'd take over.

"The Witch of Deerpath Ranch is what we used to call her," he said. "Though everybody in the family about took my head off when I said it on this trip home. Guess she's changed some."

Darby nodded, then turned toward her grandfather, silently begging him to hurry. Her brain waves must have ricocheted off his head because he began what sounded like a lecture.

"Sometimes they do that with the temperamental ones," Jonah said, "give 'em a travel mate that's gentle, let them bond before they leave, even get vaccinations and blood tests together. That way, once they're on the ship, he'd get accustomed to the different food and travel sounds and let her know everything's okay."

"From the mainland to Honolulu, it worked," Kit told them, offering Jonah the notes. "She was quiet. Didn't eat much, but that could be the switch from range forage to commercial food."

The mustang hadn't eaten much at Mrs. Allen's, either, but Darby stayed quiet. No way would she prolong this conversation.

Kit rubbed the back of his neck. "I guess it was after the quarantine that she started comin' unraveled."

Darby didn't have to puzzle this out for a second.

"She thought it was over!"

Darby felt her horse's joy at emerging from the ship's hold into the daylight. She would have tolerated the new sights, smells, even the veterinarian's touch, because she'd escaped the darkness. And then they'd forced her to go back.

A sense of betrayal tightened her throat. Every joint—shoulders, knees, ankles—stiffened against returning to the ship. And now, today, the filly was afraid it was happening all over again.

Sky all around. Earth far below. Ground changing beneath braced hooves. Far off, she caught the comforting smell of grass, but last time it had only been a trick. . . .

Darby blinked. She couldn't remember the exact moment when she'd started feeling what her horse did. She only knew, as she'd lain beside the filly in the snow, after the horse had been struck by the bus, she'd suddenly felt the filly's panic and the pang of longing for her herd.

Hooves stomped and a whinny floated to them.

"She hurt Cade, you said." Jonah's flat tone snagged Darby's attention.

"He reached for her halter and she pawed him in the chest." Kit thought for a minute. "Says he's fine and won't let me look at it. He's pretty ticked off because I pulled rank on him, wouldn't give him a second try at leading the horse out, into the trailer."

"That's your call as foreman," Jonah said.

"Yeah." Kit nodded. "It's easy to wreck wild horses. Better to let her train with someone she knows."

That means me, Darby thought, but Jonah fixed her with a look that was so analytical, he might have been sifting her cells for the "sleeping bravery" he'd attributed to her before they met.

Darby straightened her shoulders. For her filly's sake, she hoped Jonah saw what he was looking for.

"Maybe," Jonah said. "Let's go see what the horse thinks."

At last! It was all Darby could do to keep from running.

Small and skinny, the wild filly regarded her new world with a fierce glare.

The strong legs that had galloped over the range now shook as they held her upright inside the orange metal cage. Her coat was matted with sweat and straw. Her glorious mane clung dirty and greasy against her neck and her forelock hung in strings over her eyes. Those brown eyes, which had shone with intelligence in Nevada, had changed.

Darby sucked in a shuddering breath. Starvation and dirtiness could be cured, but those eyes shimmered with madness.

For a second, Darby wondered if this could be the wrong horse, but a splash of white showed on the filly's chest.

Behind Darby, someone cleared his throat and she grasped for something to say. Who could she blame for the mustang's condition? Seeing the way her horse leaned listlessly against the metal bars of her stall, Darby couldn't believe she'd bitten Kit and—what had he said?—"caught Cade a good one." Did that mean she'd kicked him?

"She's lost a lot of weight," Darby said finally.

"That happens," Jonah said, not a bit surprised. "It can take months, even a year for them to come back to what they were, but most of 'em do. For a wild horse, she's got nice size to her, really."

A month ago, Brynna, Samantha Forster's stepmom, who knew all there was to know about wild horses, had declared the filly's conformation outstanding. Brynna had pointed out the mustang's strong, graceful neck and the way it was set into her body. She'd noticed the filly's sloping shoulder, which guaranteed a smooth gait, and hindquarters packed with muscle for fast starts and stops. The mustang looked like a classic Quarter Horse, Brynna had said, except for her head, which was slightly dished like an Arabian's.

Now, despite Jonah's admiration, the filly looked shrunken. Hollows showed above her eyes and at her flanks.

But Jonah was the expert and he didn't sound worried. Both she and the filly had come across the ocean to learn from him. Maybe trusting his judgment was the first lesson.

"I'm not so sure she's a girl's horse."

The low voice wasn't Jonah's. Or Kit's. It tore Darby's glance away from her filly. Pity turned to anger as she considered the guy—who was the right age to be Cade—talking to Jonah.

Head bent in a confiding way, the guy hid his face, but Darby spotted the flashy Hawaiian flowers printed in burgundy on his Western shirt. Some cowboy.

Jonah corrected him, "I meant she *belonged* to a girl . . ."

"Not that she was suitable for one," the guy finished.

Oh, really? Darby's hands curled into fists. She had six months to make him eat those words, and she planned to begin right now.

She turned to study the filly, to see what feelings hid beneath the horse's battered exterior. Just then, the sorrel's nostrils flared, showing red as she glared at Cade. That was easy enough to read, but the filly's warning faded as her head swung toward Darby.

Recognition flashed through every line of the filly's body. First she trembled. Then her head jerked up and intelligence reclaimed her eyes. She gulped noisy breaths and her muzzle pointed straight at Darby.

"Yes," Darby whispered. A step brought her within five feet of the cage. "It's me. It's Darby. You know me."

The filly pinned her ears back, but her neck stretched, her head turned sideways, and she tried to slide her nose between the bars.

"She's gonna bite," Kit muttered, but Darby didn't believe it. She stepped close enough to feel the filly's warm breath.

Remembering the comfort of Darby's touch, the filly fought her wildness.

"Could you leave us alone?" Darby asked softly, reaching a hand toward the horse. "Please?"

The gesture and word combined were too much for the wild filly. She jumped back, striking her head on the bars. Darby winced as if the impact rung through her own skull.

"No," Kit and Jonah said together.

Their voices drew the filly's glare. With all the intensity a wild creature needed to survive, she focused on the men.

Then the mustang rolled her brown eyes until the whites showed and struck at the metal bars with her hooves.

"We'll get you out of there, girl," Darby told her. But the filly's ears didn't flicker at a tone she recognized, and the *help me* look had vanished from her eyes.

Swinging away from Darby, the mustang turned to Judge and squealed.

"She's showin' you something," Jonah told Darby.

"What?"

"Right there, she recognized you, then turned

away. If there's a choice between you and another horse, you're out of luck."

"That's all she knows," Darby said, defending the filly. "She lived her whole life with horses, not people."

Kit and Cade both looked at her grandfather.

They just let her words hang there until Jonah finally said, "Let's load 'em up."

Jonah looked at Darby, but Cade stepped forward. As he did, Darby noticed that it wasn't a Hawaiian flower print on the front of his shirt. The burgundy stain was blood.

Darby swallowed hard and considered the high-sided truck Kit had driven here. It had no top, probably so her filly wouldn't be injured if she decided to rear. Darby concentrated on the filly's safety instead of the blood on Cade, and Kit's disheveled shirt.

A month ago, she wouldn't have felt so scared, but the filly had accepted her before. She'd been through a lot since they'd met on the snowy range. If two experienced horsemen couldn't get the sorrel inside the trailer, could she?

Kit rubbed his palms together. "Now that you've calmed her down a little, we'll get the rough stuff over as quick as we can. Once you're back at the ranch, you can carry on reminding her she's no monster."

Of course the filly was no monster, and what did he mean by rough stuff?

"She's wearing a halter . . . ," Darby said slowly.

"And we got a lead rope on it. Just barely," Kit said.

"But unless they did some magic after I left the ranch, she doesn't know how to lead," Darby told them.

"Figured," Kit said, and his expression made Darby wonder if he'd had dragging rather than leading in mind.

"Load the bay," Jonah ordered Cade.

As he walked past, Darby noticed the shirt stuck to his chest. The blood was still wet, but he didn't seem to notice, as he unlatched Judge's stall door and backed him out.

Cade paused, letting Judge sniff the truck and consider it from several angles. Then, Cade walked the old bay up the ramp and into the truck.

A guttural neigh came from the filly. If there'd been room to pace, she would have, but she could only fuss, tossing her head as she jostled against the metal bars.

"Once we open the stall, will she run right into the truck to be with Judge?" Darby asked.

Braced to open the latch on the orange metal stall, Kit looked at Jonah.

"Probably, but just in case, I want you to grab hold of that lead rope," Jonah instructed.

Kit's double take told Darby he thought Jonah would be the one to approach the wild horse.

Kit gave a grunt of disagreement just as Cade said, "I can—" and Jonah cut him off by pointing at Darby.

It's all me, she thought.

The filly didn't panic at the scrutiny. Her angry huffing stopped and each intaken breath grew deeper. Relaxing, the horse dropped her head an inch and her wide-open eyelids blinked.

If they won't leave us alone, we'll make our own quiet place right here, Darby told the filly silently. *Pretend it's just the two of us.*

The filly looked into Darby's eyes as if they reflected wide Nevada skies, instead of this strange, sea-smelling place.

"She knows you." Jonah's words weren't even a whisper. "What will you do about it?"

"Take the rope, I guess."

Darby edged closer, standing in the slim space of the opening stall door. Kit's knuckles were white where he still gripped it, giving her another inch, then another.

Darby grabbed the lead rope the instant she could reach it.

Stupid! She should have moved more slowly. She'd startled the filly.

"Look out!"

Darby didn't know who said it. She watched her horse rise in a half rear. Cramped muscles flexed and the small white star, half the size of Darby's palm, glimmered on the filly's chest, showing past the sweat-stiff hair.

Not wildness, but frustration. The filly wanted to join Judge. Darby blocked the way. If she had to run through her, she would, but she gave Darby fair warning.

She couldn't let the filly run right past her. Or over her.

"Settle down, Hoku," Darby said, trying out the name.

Once more, the filly stared at her with recognition, then shuddered and turned back to Judge.

Darby held out her hand, hoping the filly would sniff it.

The sorrel's head lashed out like a striking snake's.

Darby jerked her hand back and sidestepped at the same time.

She doesn't want to be touched, that's for sure, Darby thought, but the filly's feint had been so far off target, Darby hadn't even felt a puff of air at the movement. Hoku hadn't meant to bite her—just warn her that things were different now.

The filly shifted restlessly, waiting to see what Darby did next.

"She was just threatening, wasn't she?" Darby muttered without looking away. She had to be sure.

"This time," Jonah answered.

Darby stepped backward, toe behind heel, other

toe behind other heel. The filly didn't follow until her red-amber neck reached full length. She raised a fore-foot.

"Now, get out of her way," Jonah ordered.

The filly bolted. Hooves thudded and her shoulder would have clipped Darby's if she hadn't dodged clear.

Unsure where the greater danger lay, the filly stopped half inside the truck.

"Go on. You can do it," Darby said, encouraging her.

The filly's head swung around. She stared over her shoulder. Breathing hard with confusion, she tilted her delicately shaped ears forward to catch Darby's voice.

"You're a good girl, Hoku, and soon you'll be home. Nobody will chase you with helicopters or lock you in ships or be mean to you."

The filly moved in beside Judge, pressing against his warmth, oblivious to the truck's tailgate as it closed behind her.

Dizzied by relief, Darby braced her palms against the denim covering her thighs and tried to catch a full breath.

"That name you called her," Kit said as he secured the back of the truck. "Is it Hawaiian? What does it mean?"

Darby tried to think.

"Star," Jonah supplied.

Then the truck doors slammed, and Kit and Cade were driving away with her horse.

Back in Jonah's truck, Darby realized he was determined to talk to her, even if she was too tired for it to sink in.

"Once we get back to the ranch, here's what I expect will happen," he said. "Some horses, after a trip like this, come out frolicking like foals. Others are cautious. Like her. We'll put her in a paddock that's totally secure. Something she won't get out of unless you let her out. And," he said firmly, "we'll keep her totally separate from other horses."

"No," Darby protested.

"*Yes*, and right away." He gave her a disappointed glance. "I would have thought you'd figure this out on your own. I don't think you're trying."

Figure what out? Darby thought. *That it's cruel?*

But she stayed quiet and tried to give him space. After one particularly bad weekend Darby had spent with her dad, her mom had told Darby the key to dealing with men was to give them lots of space.

So Darby watched the truck clock and gave Jonah five silent minutes. When she peeked at him again, Darby could tell Jonah wasn't any closer to backing down.

Couldn't he see she'd already gone above and beyond what anyone who knew her would expect of her? She'd traveled to Hawaii all by herself. She'd ridden—okay, at least mounted—a horse by herself.

She'd just helped load a wild filly two cowboys had failed to move. And he was disappointed in her?

This isn't about you, Darby scolded herself. *It's about Hoku.*

As they drove along, she decided to try for a compromise. "Let her have just tonight with Judge. He's the only thing that reminds her of home."

"Wrong," Jonah said. "She has you. So, you decide. Do you want Hoku to be your horse, or his?"

Chapter 7

Darby wished she could have ridden with Kit instead.

Then she could sit in the cattle truck, twist in her seat, and watch Hoku's face to gauge how the filly was doing.

But it was too late. She and Jonah drove behind the cattle truck, where she saw only a flaxen tail streaming beside a black one.

And Jonah was lecturing her. Even though he spoke in a low, conversational voice, Darby knew that was exactly what he was doing.

"What's up with you?" he asked. "Twice you should have been run down by that horse, but you weren't."

Darby was about to suggest she was just lucky when Jonah went on. "Is it because you're a horse expert?"

"No—"

"A horse psychologist, then, or maybe you just move faster than a mustang?"

"Of course not," Darby managed.

"I'll tell you why," Jonah offered.

I thought so, Darby said to herself.

"This might never happen to you again, but right here and now, you know how this horse thinks," Jonah insisted. His brows lowered, but he wore a thoughtful smile. "*Twice,* you knew what she was going to do the instant before she did it."

Why did the flowers in her lei suddenly smell too sweet? Darby coughed and rubbed at her nose. What if she was allergic to them?

"I just paid attention," Darby said, but she knew it was more than that. "Besides, she wouldn't let me touch her. Before, in Nevada, I got a halter on her and brushed her a little bit."

He drove on a few minutes before saying, "Don't waste these first few weeks when she's at her most vulnerable."

Vulnerable?

"Are you saying you think I should take advantage of her because she's in a strange place and afraid?" Darby asked.

"Yes."

I'm not like that, Darby thought.

"Everything here is new to her," Jonah said. "She's looking for a leader, to help her make sense of things."

"Judge can teach her how to be a horse—he has years of experience," Darby joked, but her attempt at humor fell flat, which was exactly the reason she rarely tried to be funny.

"You need to know more of her background," Jonah mused. "If she hasn't always been wild—"

"Some people in Nevada said she hasn't," Darby said.

"Then you'll want bloodlines and early training, all that. If she'd been purely wild, she'd have no bad habits, but if she's lived with us humans, that's another deal altogether."

"Samantha Forster said she'd investigate," Darby said. "And she'll do it."

Samantha would do anything for a horse, and so would I, but— Darby's thoughts broke off when she felt an ache in her hands. She looked down to see them clenched in such tight fists, her knuckles were white with pale-pink lines. Why was she afraid to work with Hoku?

Because I'm a wimp, she thought. This wasn't like school. She could do school. And even if she got behind or distracted, even if she earned a low score on a test, she could study hard and catch up. Here, everything was different.

That plane from Oahu had set her down on an island where the test was putting what she knew into action. What if she reached down to pull up the "sleeping bravery" she needed, and there was nothing there? Would she mess up this beautiful, frightened horse?

Jonah didn't say anything. Maybe he was as worn out as she was, and ready for this roller-coaster day to end.

But I rode Navigator all by myself, Darby thought, and couldn't help grinning out the window at the green grass and green trees.

Green plants even pushed up through the asphalt road, and Darby realized she didn't know the name of one of them. She wasn't doing that well with the people, either.

Tonight, before she fell asleep, she'd have to get out her little notebook and write stuff down.

Kimo's name was easy to remember. Kit Ely, she'd already heard about. There was Cade and Cathy, but she couldn't remember Cathy's daughter's name.

My mind was on Hoku, Darby thought, excusing herself. And there'd been a good reason for it. Hoku had been swinging through the air in that cage, landing on the docks, and defending herself against strange humans.

Darby stared out the truck window and yawned. She wondered what her best friend Heather was doing right now.

Maybe swimming. She and Heather had taken lessons together for years and they'd agreed on a goal. The summer they turned sixteen, they'd both be lifeguards. Darby was imagining herself with slick, wet hair and a red swimsuit, tweeting her whistle at rowdy swimmers, when the ranch dogs' greeting barks interrupted and Jonah's Land Rover bumped down the dirt road.

Later, Darby stood at the fence of a paddock halfway between the house and the arena and watched Hoku tremble.

Once, Kimo walked up to see the filly. She flattened her ears and swung her head to drive him away.

"Not ready for company, are you?" he concluded. "But you're gonna have to put up with me for a second."

Kimo wound a brown bungee cord twice around the gate, then fastened the two hooked ends.

"Kit's idea," Kimo said as he met Darby's questioning look. "He tells me mustangs don't jump. They run through fences." His eyes gave the filly a quick once-over. "Me? I think a wild horse might have more sense than a tame one, but this bolt on the gate is old. No harm in a little extra security."

Kimo went back to work, but Hoku knew exactly where he'd stood, and she stayed farther away from that spot than the rest of the fence.

Not long after that, Hoku spotted Cade leaving the ranch yard on a jogging Appaloosa. Hoku bolted, as if she'd run after them.

Mustangs don't jump. They run through fences. That's what Kimo had said. Kit had told him that and Kit knew wild horses.

Darby could hardly breathe. Hoku's chest would strike and break the fence. It could shatter into huge splinters.

"No!" Darby shouted.

The filly swerved with just inches to spare, then trotted along the fence with her head held high. Her beseeching neigh called for Judge, wherever he was, begging him to return. Her pleas went on and on, endless and ear-splitting, but Darby stood there and took the assault on her eardrums. At least she could do that to show the filly that they belonged together.

Dusk fell around Darby. Her shirt was soaked by a warm drizzle. She should go in and change. But once inside, she'd have to talk to the people who were her hosts.

An urgency that had to do with manners and finding out where she'd be sleeping, eating, and reading made Darby's stomach tighten. She had to go up to the house and find Cathy or Jonah, but she couldn't ignore Hoku's sign of trust as the filly drifted a few steps closer.

Hoku relaxed, stretching as if she enjoyed the

warm rain on her travel-tight muscles.

"Not like the storms at home, is it, girl?" Darby asked.

The filly startled away as if Darby had spoken in a snake's hiss or cougar's growl.

"Silly girl," she said to Hoku in a teasing way. "You remember me."

Wide-eyed, Hoku watched Darby, then tossed her head. Her throat vibrated in silence before she uttered another lonely neigh. When an answer came from one of the faraway pastures, Hoku froze, then kicked her hind legs and made three galloping circuits of the paddock, looking for a way out.

Around Darby, people did chores, came home from school, slammed car doors, and shooed a horse away from some bagged feed. Vaguely, she identified a rushing, tinkling sound as someone pouring dog chow into aluminum bowls.

Suddenly, Hoku stopped neighing. Sidestepping with ears flattened, Hoku gazed past Darby. The sorrel trotted to the far side of the paddock as boots crunched, and Kimo's voice made Darby turn.

"The horses who worked get carrots at the end of the day. Navigator hasn't had his yet."

The big horse followed Kimo at a walk, snorting and tossing his forelock.

Darby took a carrot from Kimo. She used both hands to break it. It was the sort of big woody carrot her mother avoided in the grocery store, but

Navigator savored it with closed eyes, then bumped Darby's wrist for a second one.

"Only one carrot for the first horse I ever rode in my whole life. It's a scandal, all right," she told him.

"You did okay today," Kimo said.

"Thanks," Darby answered.

When she'd first met him in the airport, Kimo had reminded her of a square stone house, but now she knew there was nothing hard about him.

His small compliment made her feel like jumping in the air to click her heels together. "Okay" sounded like "fantastic" when she applied it to mounting a horse for the first time.

His praise made her feel proud and eager to do more.

"I can't wait for tomorrow," she told him. "Then I can ride him for real, can't I?"

"Sure," he said. He pulled the collar of his shirt up a little to ward off a drizzle, which had turned into rain. He leaned his palms on the top fence rail.

The filly's head was lowered and rain dripped off her nose. Darby braced herself. If Kimo said something about the filly looking scrawny and miserable, he'd only be telling the truth.

But he didn't.

"Hoku, huh?" Kimo said. "I know two girls named Hoku. A guy, too, used to play football with me."

"So she'll fit right in," Darby said, spirits lifting.

He nodded, and Darby savored the idea.

"Cathy wants you at the house for dinner. Jonah and Kit are cleaned up and hungry, I guess. Megan — have you met her yet? Sometimes we call her Mekana. Nice girl. Anyway, I told them I'd let you know before I left."

Suddenly, she remembered Cathy telling Jonah she'd planned a welcome dinner for Darby. *That's* what had been gnawing at her. Great. She was late and looked like a half-drowned chicken.

What did her mom always say? You only had one chance to make a first impression. Darby hoped that since everyone here lived with horses and cared about them, they'd excuse her putting Hoku's needs above proper etiquette.

Looking through the rain, Darby noticed lights shining yellow from inside the house. "What time is it?"

"Late. With Kit and Cade gone most of the day, it took longer to get things done."

Why didn't someone ask me to help? Darby wondered.

Kimo squinted down the road as if he could see all the way to his home at the lip of the waterfall valley. "Better go. My dad's already given my dinner to the hogs."

Darby hoped he was joking.

"Get Mekana to put that lei in the refrigerator for you, and later you can give it back to the ocean," Kimo said.

"Okaayy," Darby drew the word out, confused.

How could you give the lei "back" to the ocean, when the flowers certainly weren't aquatic?

"If you do that," Kimo explained, "you'll return to the islands."

"Return?" Darby yelped. "I just got here. I'm not going anyplace else. Not without my horse."

Kimo glanced up at the house and tugged his hat brim lower against the rain.

"That's what you say," he told her, and Darby was pretty sure he was joking when he added, "but the day's not over yet."

As Kimo drove away, Darby left the horses and walked toward the house that was supposed to become her home.

The door stood open. Voices, along with the clink of silverware and glass, drifted out with the aroma of exotic food. Even though she wasn't really cold, the warmth inside Sun House tempted her to leave the drizzle and enter.

She stepped into a cluttered tile foyer. Just ahead, beige carpet led down a hall on her left. Three closed doors probably meant two bedrooms and a bathroom. On her right —

"There you are!" Cathy greeted Darby. She wore a blue beach skirt and flowers in her hair. Even though her arms were full of dishes, she gave Darby a kiss on each cheek.

Should she kiss her back? Darby's arms hung at

her sides and she had no idea.

Finally she touched the book in her pocket and realized it was wet. All the time she'd stood in the rain . . . how could she have forgotten it? She snatched the book from her pocket and fanned its pages.

"It'll be all right," Cathy said. "The paper might be a little wavy, but everything that gets wet here eventually dries out."

Darby looked up. The sympathy in Cathy's voice was reflected in her gentle expression.

She thinks I'm a nutcase, Darby realized, and sifted her thoughts for something normal to say. She fell back on the last thing Kimo had told her to do. Touching her flower lei, she asked, "Can I put this in the refrigerator?"

"Absolutely. Let me do it for you." Cathy shifted the stack of dishes to one arm so she could take the lei.

Why hadn't Darby noticed that Cathy was busy putting dinner on the table? Not that it mattered now. Cathy had already stowed the garland and set the dishes down on a counter.

"Let's go see your room," she said, then waved Darby down the hall ahead of her. She stopped at the door at the end of the hall and opened it.

The snug room smelled of fresh paint and its white walls shone with it.

They fixed this room up just for me, Darby thought.

The polished wood floor was the color of peanut

butter. A twin bed covered with a tufted white bedspread sat under a window angled so that she could see the ranch yard. A glossy black headboard matched two bedside tables, a desk, and a bookcase.

"Wow, thanks," Darby said. She kicked herself for not being able to come up with a more gracious reaction.

"I'm glad you like it," Cathy said as Darby moved toward a clay vase holding a spindly green plant.

"What's this?" Darby asked, lifting it.

"Lucky bamboo," Cathy said.

"I like it," Darby said. It would be cool to have something living in the room with her.

"You're going to need it if you keep all those hungry people waiting," Cathy told her.

"Sorry!"

"Usually Kit and Cade don't eat with us, and since—" Cathy broke off. Sadness changed her eyes, but she shook her head, refusing to let it get a grip on her. *"Lately,"* she corrected herself, "dinner hasn't been too organized. Now that there are four of us living in the house, we're going to have real dinners again every night."

"I'm not picky," Darby assured her.

"Can you cook? Because I think we'll be taking turns," Cathy rushed on before Darby could answer. Then, she caught Darby's glance toward her packed suitcases, and added, "Don't bother changing. Just wash your hands. As I said, we're pretty informal around here."

"I'll hurry," Darby said.

Hoku's neigh floated in through the open window, and Darby paused in her rush to the bathroom down the hall. She sent her horse a mental message.

Soon, baby. The minute I can escape, I'll come to you.

When Darby had washed her hands, she glanced into the mirror over the bathroom sink. She saw Cathy's reflection, just the back of her bobbed hair as she waited for Darby and looked down the hall toward the kitchen.

Darby made a hasty attempt to smooth fallen tendrils of hair toward her ponytail. Then she plucked the damp, clinging shirt away from her ribs and turned from the mirror.

"This way," Cathy said. She curled her arm around Darby's shoulders, led her down the hall, then drew her into a room open to the sky.

"Dinner's on the lanai," Cathy explained as she steered Darby toward an outdoor table where Jonah, Kit, and a girl about her own age stood waiting.

Lanai? Darby thought of recording the new word in her notebook, but only wondered what had become of it for a minute, because from this lanai, she could see . . . everything.

Kit and Jonah stood at the rail, talking and looking out at the pastures below.

The view worked like a magnet, pulling Darby forward, until she overheard the men's conversation.

"Don't know that I've ever been so wrong about a horse," Jonah muttered. "Range rats, isn't that what they call 'em?"

Darby stopped.

"Some do. I'm more inclined to say they're suited to the high desert."

Thank you, Kit, Darby thought. Kit wanted Jonah to give Hoku a chance.

Could Jonah feel her glare searing his back?

When he slapped his hand on the lanai railing as though Kit had made a joke, Darby's anger blazed up. His laugh might as well have been gasoline poured on a fire.

Lucky the Hawaiian horse charmer couldn't read *her* mind, because she'd just pictured him tumbling off the lanai and rolling down the hill.

Darby's face burned with a hot blush. Scared or not, she had to stand up for Hoku. But what should she say?

Just then, Cathy snagged her elbow and whispered, "He's bluffing, setting low expectations, so people are amazed later."

I don't know. Darby hesitated with lips already parted.

Cathy knew Jonah better than she did. Still . . .

"Besides," Jonah said, chuckling, "I can't afford to walk away from a two-thousand-dollar mistake."

Two thousand dollars was what it had cost Jonah to bring Hoku to Hawaii.

Cathy cleared her throat and both men turned around.

Darby noticed that Kit had taken time to put on fresh jeans and a black shirt with gray snaps. The crisply ironed shirt nearly covered chunks of turquoise strung on leather around his neck.

Kit also wore an embarrassed expression.

Not Jonah. One eyebrow was raised higher than the other. Beneath his black mustache, his mouth was awfully close to a smile.

Startled, Darby wondered, *Did he know all along that I was standing there, listening?*

He motioned her closer and Darby took a grudging step.

"Come see this view, Granddaughter," he said. "It's exactly what you'd see if you were an angel hovering over paradise."

Darby couldn't help looking. As Jonah pointed out twin volcanoes called Two Sisters and the snow-covered peak he said most people called Sky Mountain, she heard his love for this land.

Jonah was the most confusing human she'd ever met, Darby thought, then her stomach growled at the scent of food.

"Dinnertime," Jonah said, and nodded toward the table.

A platter of barbecued meat sat amid bowls of rice, macaroni salad, and a huge platter of sliced fruit. Colorful napkins and flowers made it look like a celebration.

"Darby, this is my daughter Megan," Cathy said, giving the girl who stood next to her a shoulder squeeze.

Megan was taller than her mother and she radiated fitness. She belonged in a magazine advertisement for athletic shoes or protein bars, Darby thought.

They both said "Hi," but Darby was pretty sure Megan hated her on sight.

Okay, that was an overstatement, but Megan looked cool. And Darby knew that she *wasn't* cool, and probably never would be.

Besides her glowing good health, Megan had russet hair cut in an actual style. She wore tan capris and a fashionable top, not jeans and a rumpled shirt. Instead of muddy boots, Megan's feet were bare and her toenails sparkled with pink polish.

Darby froze. Everyone but her had left their shoes near the door. Everyone. Even Kit the Nevada cowboy was bootless. Had she violated a local custom? Would it be better to go take her boots off now, or just ignore her mistake?

"It's nice to meet you," Megan said. "It'll be fun having another girl around."

She said it so warmly, Darby suspected Megan had seen her discomfort and taken pity on her. But that was okay.

"I'm glad to meet you, too," Darby said.

As she settled into her chair, Darby's eyes darted down the table. Jonah sat at one end and Cathy sat at the other. There were six place settings.

Cade was missing, though Cathy had said he was invited. After all, Jonah had called him his foster son.

Darby gave a mental shrug, and just enjoyed the relief that she'd start her new school knowing at least one person. Megan.

Maybe, if they got to be friends, she could ask Megan questions about island life that she'd be embarrassed to put to anyone else.

"Cade's late," Cathy said, sounding surprised.

"Thought you knew. I sent him out to ride fence and work off his bad mood," Jonah said.

Bad mood over what? Darby wondered, but her question went unasked, because Cathy had changed the subject.

"You'll have to see Darby's horse," Cathy said as Megan took the seat across from Darby. When Megan just contemplated her empty plate, Cathy added, "The filly's a wild Nevada mustang, maybe the first one in Hawaii, right, Jonah?"

Jonah skimmed over the question to tell Darby, "Megan's a good rider."

Instead of beaming, Megan repositioned her silverware and said, "I used to ride."

Cathy looked pained by her daughter's remark and Jonah shifted in his chair, but the uneasiness only lasted a few seconds.

Darby ate and forced herself to ignore the voice in her head that kept repeating "range rat" and "two-thousand-dollar mistake."

She concentrated as Cathy explained Sun House had once been a plantation house.

Although she'd never been in any mansion, this Hawaiian plantation house made of wood and open to warm breezes on every side was sure different from the pillared Southern structure the word brought to Darby's mind.

Kit and Jonah drifted into a conversation about fencing.

"We have wood instead of wire," Jonah told Darby. "It's one thing I insist on, no matter the cost."

During their drive from the airport, Kimo had mentioned that their neighbors—the Zinks, was it?—used barbed wire.

Was Jonah's superior tone directed at those neighbors? Why didn't Megan ride anymore? And what had made Cade so angry?

Trying to soak up facts about her new home

wasn't easy with all these undercurrents, but Darby managed to notice the men called the pastures by names. Instead of saying "the south forty" the way she'd read farmers did, they called one Borderlands and another Sugar Mill.

When she glanced up and accidentally met Megan's gaze, the other girl rolled her eyes in mock boredom. But when Cathy took the cover from a small plate she'd kept next to her, Megan gasped, "Mom! You made candy?"

"Macadamia brittle," Cathy said, as if it was no big deal. "See what you think."

"It's great," Megan said before she'd even taken a bite. "But it's been so long since, you know, you made it."

Darby thought the candy was outstanding, but her second piece became hard to swallow when Jonah said, "Tell us how you came to have Hoku."

Darby told herself that since she hadn't entered any of the conversations going on around her, Jonah was just trying to draw her out and make her part of the group. But hadn't her mom talked to him about how she'd met her filly? And after what he'd said about Hoku being a range rat, did he really want to know?

"Please," Jonah said, leaning back in his chair.

Though Darby didn't like the idea of being the after-dinner entertainment, she couldn't say, *There's not much to tell.* It wasn't true, and it was unfair to Hoku.

Her mind drifted outside. She imagined her horse enjoying the tropical rain, and then Darby shivered, remembering the snow.

Chapter 8

Darby could almost feel the icy wind seeping around the window of the school bus that had picked her up at the Reno Airport after she'd flown in from Los Angeles. She remembered staring out and being surprised that snow didn't fall in crystalline flakes, as she'd read it did. In northern Nevada, it had dropped from the sky in clumps that got bigger as they bumped into one another and stuck. She'd never seen snow before and she'd wondered how something so beautiful could make her so miserable.

Shivering in the nylon windbreaker she'd only worn because her mom had nagged her into it, she'd tried not to breathe in. The air was so cold it scraped her lungs like knives.

When a mechanical racket outside finally distracted Darby from shivering, Samantha Forster pointed out the helicopter circling like a vulture, and told her it was searching for wild horses.

Darby still tried to keep her eyes lowered to her book.

She'd been so embarrassed by the fact that that Sam Forster had instantly become her role model. Sam was a real cowgirl who lived on a ranch, was a counselor for Dream Catcher Wild Horse Camp, and knew all about the range and the battle over the West's mustangs.

Samantha had instantly known Darby loved horses, too. Sam had even confided that she had a special bond with a wild silver stallion.

Darby remembered trying to be skeptical, but the melancholy and pride in Sam's eyes had convinced Darby that Sam was telling the truth.

When a helicopter pilot had swooped low enough to cast blue shadows on the snow, he'd flushed two horses out of a canyon.

"I see them!" Darby had yelled.

One horse was dark brown and one was golden sorrel. They galloped with a fairy-tale grace she'd never imagined. The sorrel's hooves floated above the snow. Full of her own speed, she gloried not in escape, but in the pleasure of running. If Darby's whole trip had ended then, it would have been worth all the arguments, money, and cold.

But suddenly the bus had begun sliding. One instant the openmouthed horses were close enough that Darby saw patches of sweat on their coats. The next second, they disappeared.

"Stop!" Sam had screamed.

The bus driver had yelled a warning before Darby's world turned upside down, sideways, and upside down again.

"And then what?" Cathy gasped, bringing Darby back to the lanai, the table, the candles.

"After that, I guess I was kind of out of it," Darby told them. "I remember broken glass and the bus driver's head bleeding and Sam Forster totally taking charge."

"Those ranch girls are like that," Kit said approvingly.

Megan and her mother met each other's eyes.

"Of course we are," Cathy said, then motioned Darby to go on.

"I helped take care of the bus driver. Head wounds bleed a lot, you know, so I applied direct pressure and covered him with an emergency blanket and stuff."

A shout of laughter came from Jonah and they all looked at him. Grinning, he passed the fingers of both hands through the gray hair at his temples and chuckled. "I like that."

Even though she was a city girl, she'd done what she could, Darby thought, and looking back on it, she kind of liked that part, too. Under Sam's direction, she'd stepped up and taken care of a man in need.

"Tell us about the horse," Megan said, and Darby sighed.

"It was love at first sight," Kit filled in for her.

He might have been kidding, but Darby nodded.

Then she remembered the awful, smothered shriek that had come from outside the bus.

At first she'd thought it was the bus driver, but when she and Sam finally escaped the bus, it was something worse.

"She was half under the bus and she was making an awful sound," Darby said.

She didn't look at the others for sympathy, just pictured Hoku's hooves flailing grooves in the snow. Her tail had fanned across the whiteness beneath her, and her nostrils had flared to reveal red veins.

"I begged Sam to help her, but it was a stupid thing to do. When she heard me talking, Hoku got all desperate to escape."

Darby remembered how her voice had scared the sorrel. She'd plunged her forelegs forward and lashed her head around, teeth bared as she glared through skeins of pale mane and forelock. Then she'd collapsed, head flat against the snow, eyes wide as they looked into Darby's.

Darby's arms had clamped around herself as though she could hold in a heart that might shatter.

Fear had clawed every nerve. Panic made her

still, as if she could disappear into the snow. For several minutes, Darby's thoughts had confused her. Only as Sam left her in charge and walked down the long cold highway for help did Darby realize the fear wasn't hers, but the horse's.

Darby didn't mention that part now.

Kit sat on the other side of the table, so when he tilted his head to one side, Darby could tell he wanted to ask something, but he hesitated.

"So then Samantha left for help," Darby said.

"Yeah, but . . ." Kit began, then rubbed his wrist and looked at it a few seconds. "Don't know if he made this up, mind you, but my brother Jake told me you laid right down in the snow with that filly."

"In the snow?" Megan asked.

Staring past Kit, over the lanai railing, off the bluff into the darkness full of horses, Darby tried to explain. "I tried to think like a horse. I figured if I was her and I'd grown up in a herd, I'd want someone close to me when I was hurt. And I thought I might be less scary to her if I wasn't standing up like I was going to pounce or something, so . . ."

"So you laid down in the snow and covered the horse with the only blanket," Kit said. "That's what I heard, but you really did?" He turned to the others apologetically. "I believe Darby. It's just that . . . I've been around those wild ones and I can't picture that working for me."

The last thing Darby wanted was for Megan and her mom to start looking at her weirdly, as Jonah had this afternoon. She was no wild-horse witch.

"There were actually two blankets," Darby said, correcting him.

"You covered the bus driver with one," Cathy put in.

Darby nodded. She'd been talking for too long and she wanted to stop, but they were all waiting for the end of the story, so she said, "Then I just talked to her, really quietly."

It would sound silly if she told them she'd thought of all the small sounds—nickers and snorts and stamps—she imagined horses made when they bedded down together in a herd, and filled in comforting noises with her own voice.

"And she stayed calm?" Cathy asked.

"She did fine until people started coming," Darby said.

"You say that—*people*—like you're not one of them," Megan pointed out. "I mean one of *us*," Megan said, and when she laughed at herself, Darby smiled.

"You gotta admit, they did save you from hypothermia," Kit said.

"I know," Darby agreed. "But they were being so loud, and I was looking right in Hoku's eyes and all the fear that had gone out of them was coming back and I—"

Darby broke off. There were some things you didn't share with strangers. Even if one of them was your grandfather.

She hadn't told her mother and she wouldn't tell anyone else that Mrs. Allen had said, "You growled at us to stay back, just like a mother bear!"

"I'd say you were pretty brave." Cathy stood and began gathering plates.

Everyone rose slowly, as if they were just waking up.

"Nice dinner, Mom," Megan said, collecting plates and silverware and following her mother toward the kitchen.

"A great meal," Jonah agreed, but his eyes stayed on Darby.

"Can I help?" Darby asked.

"Tomorrow," Cathy called back to her.

"Thanks for includin' me," Kit said. "Sometime, I'll whip up a batch of Nevada chili and feed you all." Then Kit touched Darby's elbow and lowered his voice to say, "No wonder that filly trusts you. You guarded her when she was surrounded by human beasts, just like the lead mare in her herd would. You made yourself part of her family."

Darby took a deep breath. Kit had grown up in wild horse country. He knew what he was talking about.

She met her grandfather's eyes and saw Jonah had heard Kit.

She's looking for a leader, someone to teach her.

You made yourself part of her family.

First Jonah, and now Kit. Two horsemen believed she was Hoku's best chance to be happy. If Hoku forgot the confined and confusing sea journey and recalled that hour in the snow, maybe it *could* be true.

Darby bit her lip and considered Jonah. He stood at the front door, watching Kit go.

She wanted to ask Jonah if she could have Hoku all to herself, with no interruptions. Surely there was someplace on this huge ranch where it could be just the two of them. It was the right thing to do and she knew it.

So what was she afraid of?

Not Jonah. He'd separated the filly from Judge and the other horses and told her to take advantage of Hoku's vulnerability.

Not Hoku. She loved the filly with all her heart and so far, she'd been able to anticipate her risky moves.

Darby yawned and decided there'd be time to psychoanalyze herself later.

"Mom! You're telling me she doesn't have to go to school?" Megan's shocked voice carried to Darby from the kitchen.

"Not right away," Cathy answered.

"You've got to be kidding!" Megan's tone could've held envy or pity.

Either way, Darby understood her reaction. Why *wouldn't* she be going to school? Darby would bet there was only one person who knew.

"It's not up to me, honey," Cathy said.

Darby watched Jonah close the front door. He strode toward the kitchen, crooking a finger at Darby to indicate she should follow along.

Like one of the ranch dogs, Darby protested silently. But she managed to say, "I am going to school, right?"

"Don't get excited over nothing," Jonah said, and kept walking.

Excited? She was totally calm and reasonable! And she wasn't about to "heel" into the kitchen.

For a few seconds, then a whole minute, Darby stood with her feet braced.

Jonah, Cathy, and Megan were in there talking about her. She could hear them. But not very well.

Darby moaned in frustration and rushed into the kitchen in time for Jonah to ask,

"You're smart, right?"

"Pretty smart," she said cautiously.

"Pretty smart," he repeated with a you-can-do-better-than-that look.

"Okay, yeah. I'm smart," Darby said, but Jonah sighed in mock boredom. She added, "I read above my grade level."

The kitchen was so quiet, Darby heard hooves trotting up and down, back and forth.

They were Hoku's. Darby just knew it. She sifted through what she'd learned of Jonah so far, and tried to answer in a way that would get her out of here the quickest.

"I read at college level," she admitted. Jonah's raised eyebrow prodded her on. "And I'm not bad at history or science."

Jonah didn't look happier.

Darby glanced to Megan. When she saw that the other girl appeared interested, not annoyed by Darby's admission that she was smart, the words came tumbling out.

"I'm okay at math, but I'm awful at sports and doing things with my hands. I still have nightmares about dodgeball, and don't get me started about the basket-weaving project I had to do in fourth grade!"

"Oh my gosh! Me too," Megan crowed. "And *she*"—Megan jabbed a finger Cathy's way—"made me learn to crochet."

"Clearly child abuse." Cathy's sigh made both girls laugh.

Hoku's neigh soared through the kitchen window.

Jonah's head and shoulders swung toward the door as if someone had knocked.

"Go check on your horse," he said. "She needs to know you haven't left her."

Darby ran out of the kitchen, through the entrance hall, and shouldered through the half-open door into the night.

Even though there'd been no urgency in Jonah's voice, Darby hurried. She leaped off the porch, stumbled, ignored the heavy feeling in her chest, and managed to stay on her feet.

Hoku had stopped neighing, but Darby rushed through the warm night as if she were a horse herself, summoned by a member of her herd.

As she ran up the knoll toward Hoku's corral, Darby's thigh muscles tugged, reminding her how she'd thrown her leg over Navigator's back.

The drizzle had stopped, but wind had slammed the door behind her as she left the house and now it pulled her hair out straight, like a mustang's mane, as she ran.

Claws skittered in the dirt. Something big was panting.

Predators were part of a horse's life that she'd rather not face. But Jonah wouldn't have sent her into a night where wild jungle beasts prowled, would he?

Sucking in her stomach and holding her arms close to her body, Darby made herself a smaller target. Then she darted toward the tack room, luring whatever it was away from Hoku's corral.

She ran a dozen strides or so, then turned to confront the creature.

It was still coming.

Darby heard panting. She squinted through the darkness, making out the silhouettes of a pack of —

Dogs.

They attacked her, all right. With wet noses and licking tongues, they bounded around, asking her to play.

"You . . ." Hands on her hips, Darby barely pronounced the accusing word before she tilted her head back and struggled for a breath.

I'm not wheezing, she told herself. *I'm just not good at running.*

She motioned for the dogs to follow her and walked slowly back up the knoll. The pack of Australian shepherds followed happily, but the little white dog growled a complaint.

Hoku bolted to the far side of the corral when she saw Darby and the dogs coming. Her ears pricked forward, interested rather than terrified.

"Shh," Darby hushed the dogs.

Wind blew through the trees. A flock of birds somersaulted overhead, swept along by the wind. Over by the bunkhouse something pinged. But the sound was too regular to be menacing.

Adrenaline drained out of Darby, leaving her weak. She sagged against the fence, then let herself down to the ground and sat watching Hoku.

A nicker rumbled low in the filly's chest.

"You're a long way from home, aren't you, pretty girl?" she asked.

But Hoku hadn't run out of energy the way Darby had. The filly swept into a galloping round of the paddock.

Darby started to laugh, but it turned into a cough. She *was* wheezing, after all.

She looked around, sneaked the inhaler from her pocket, and took a puff of it. Everyone around her seemed so healthy and fit. She didn't want them to think she was a weakling.

"It's those Kona winds."

Darby might have yelped in surprise if the dogs hadn't all risen to their feet an instant before Jonah spoke.

"Those winds are full of volcanic ash. At least, that's what my dad told me when I had asthma."

Even though it was childish, Darby felt a pulse of satisfaction because they shared something. But she only said, "I'm fine."

"Sure. You'll outgrow it like I did," Jonah said.

Darby didn't talk again until her breathing had settled down, and Jonah didn't seem to care. Together they watched Hoku watch them.

"So why don't you want me to go to school?" Darby asked Jonah finally.

"I do, but settle in here for a couple weeks. Learn to ride, to help out with chores," Jonah said. "Then go to school."

Darby's devotion to school had always been single-minded and rigid. Her attendance was nearly perfect. Reading and studying were the things she excelled at.

And yet here was her grandfather, the paniolo.

His bloodlines went back through generations of Hawaiian cowboys to those who'd taken the name paniolo from Hispaniola, in honor of the vaqueros who'd taught them to rope and ride.

Her mom had claimed that Jonah knew horses and riding as few people did.

Heart thumping, Darby realized she really did have a heritage of horses, and Jonah, gruff and harsh as he was, wanted to teach her. His "school" held a real risk that she'd fall on her face, literally and figuratively, but she loved horses, and Hoku most of all. Shouldn't she grab this chance to learn how to be more than her filly's owner?

"When would I go to school?" Darby pressed him.

"When you're ready," Jonah said.

Darby looked toward her horse. Moonlight glimmered on the filly's intelligent eyes as she watched the humans.

Surprised by her decision, by her willingness to take a chance if it would help Hoku, Darby nodded and told her grandfather, "Okay."

Chapter 9

Sun-dancing leaves made shadows on Darby's bed-room wall.

There wasn't a clock in her room, but the pastel light made her think it was early.

She stretched her toes toward the end of her bed. Achy muscles felt good when they came from doing something as wonderful as riding. She'd been up late, too.

After her mom had called to check on her, Jonah had let Darby stay up until midnight.

Her mom never would have allowed Darby to crouch in the dirt with Kona winds blowing volcanic ash into her lungs, after she'd had to take her asthma medicine. But Darby didn't plan on telling her.

So that she didn't forget any of the things she did want to tell her mother, Darby grabbed her notebook, flopped on her tummy, and jotted down the names of everyone—human and animal—she'd met the day before. Then she put in a sort of pronunciation guide.

What else? She waggled the pen between her fingers, before adding places: Crimson Vale, Two Sisters volcanoes, and Sky Mountain.

Her mom had urged her to call Mrs. Allen at the Blind Faith Mustang Sanctuary in Nevada and thank her for sending Judge along to keep Hoku company. Darby had done her best to wheedle her mom into calling. It wasn't that Darby didn't want to talk to Mrs. Allen—but she wasn't sure she could get up the nerve to ask Jonah for permission to make a long-distance call. Her mom had insisted it was Darby's job.

This morning, with her energy restored, Darby figured as long as she was asking, she'd see if she could call Sam, too.

When Samantha Forster had told her about the silver stallion she called the Phantom, Darby had envied their bond, and that's what she wanted for herself and Hoku. Sam and her brainy best friend Jen were supposed to be finding out all they could about Hoku. Darby just hoped Sam and Jen had time to do the research.

When she'd been in Nevada, there had been an awful lot of excitement going on. A neighbor named

Linc Slocum had been arrested, Jen's family had come into a bunch of money, and Sam's little brother Cody had been born at home during a huge snowstorm.

A warm gust of air lifted her curtains, bringing Darby back to the present, and all at once, the description of someone with "get-up-and-go" made sense. She had it, big time.

Swinging her legs out of bed, Darby bounced to her feet and rummaged in her suitcase for riding clothes. She should put all this stuff in drawers, but that could wait.

Darby was pulling on an orange T-shirt when the floorboards overhead creaked and a screeching hair dryer reminded her that Megan and her mom lived upstairs. It was kind of weird, but Darby didn't remember seeing a staircase.

Dressed and headed through her bedroom door, Darby backtracked for her notebook. She slipped it into a front pocket where it wouldn't interfere with riding.

Riding. She loved how her life had changed in the last twenty-four hours.

She grabbed her gray hooded sweatshirt, tugged it on, and stashed a book in the front pocket.

Then she left her room, trying to tame her grin; Megan was going to school and she wasn't.

Don't gloat, Darby told herself. She emerged from

the hall, glanced toward the living room, and her sense of celebration cranked up even more.

So this was why Jonah called his home Sun House.

Dawn crested like a wave on the horizon, haloing the forest before it spilled over the hills, then splashed honey-colored light onto the lanai and into the living room.

Darby twirled in her own personal sunbeam. She might have burst into a dance if she hadn't noticed Cathy Kato standing in the kitchen doorway, sipping coffee.

"Settling in?" she asked with an understanding smile.

Darby nodded, but Cathy's warmth coaxed her to talk. "Today, I'm spending every minute with the horses."

"Make sure you eat something before you head out." Cathy beckoned her into the kitchen. "There's cold cereal, toast, and milk."

"And yogurt."

Darby stepped aside as Megan, spooning pink yogurt from a carton, sidled through the doorway from behind her.

"Where did you come from?" Darby asked. "Is there a hidden staircase?"

"Sort of," Megan said. She darted a glance at her mother. "Our apartment has a private entrance. The stairs go up the side of the house."

"How cool!" Darby said. "I'd love to have a room like that!"

"Well, we—you, uh—"

When Megan shot a guilty glance at her mother, Darby wondered if the other girl thought she was trying to move in on them.

"I like my room," Darby insisted, and then Cathy rescued her tongue-tied daughter by bustling between the two girls.

Cranking the water on to a loud splatter, she rinsed out a bowl and said, "Breakfast is pretty much self-serve around here."

"That's fine," Darby replied. Even though she wasn't hungry, she poured a bowl of cereal. How lame would it be if hunger lured her back from her ride?

Car keys jingled.

"I'm the school bus," Cathy told Darby. "And we're twenty miles from town, so we need to get going. If you want anything, Jonah's out there some-where and Kit will be bringing up horses. Kimo should be along any time."

Megan slung a pink and black backpack over one shoulder and headed out the door behind her mother. "See you after school," she called.

Darby waited for the Land Rover to drive off before going to check on Hoku.

As she stepped outside, she saw Jonah and Kit standing near the tack shed with two horses.

Feeling shy, Darby paused and took out her notebook. She sketched a little map of the ranch and remembered thinking, yesterday, that the arrangement of buildings looked like open arms.

The land was kind of like an arm, too. Her pencil flew as she sketched the terrain to resemble a gently bent arm with Sun House up at the shoulder, the tack room and bunkhouse in the smooth inside of the elbow, Hoku's paddock at the slanted-up forearm, and the arena in the plateau of the hand.

Lips pressed together, she showed the road striking out from the right side of the elbow. Though she hadn't explored it yet, Darby glanced up, then down, and drew a dirt path leading from the left of the elbow, past a ramshackle building and on to another corral.

When she looked up again, trying to see where the Zink ranch bordered 'Iolani, Kit gave a wave.

No more stalling. Darby stowed her notebook in her pocket, pulled up her hood, and walked toward them with the little white dog sniffing at her heels.

Hoku was quiet in her paddock, but the filly's presence drew Darby. She wanted to go up there, but Kit was brushing Navigator with brisk strokes, maybe for her, so it would be pretty rude to walk on past.

"Mornin'," Kit greeted her, with a nod.

"Hi," Darby said.

Jonah set down the hoof of a gangly buckskin horse. "Call the farrier," he muttered to Kit, "and bring up the stock that needs shoes."

"Yes, boss," Kit said.

Jonah brushed his palms together, then turned to Darby.

"You'll learn to saddle up. Ride around and get a sense of where you are. First, though, check on your filly. Let the dogs out on your way."

"Right," Darby said. He sure gave a lot of orders.

It didn't take her long to figure out the flip lock on the kennel, but the dogs barked impatiently while she did. When the gate opened, they bounded after her as she hurried toward Hoku.

The filly stood against the farthest fence, on the single patch of dirt in her grassy pen. Hoku looked better this morning, Darby thought. Some of the travel grime had disappeared from her coat, mane, and tail.

"C'mere, girl," Darby called softly.

Hoku's ears flicked at the sound of Darby's voice, but she didn't look at her. Even when Darby made a clucking sound, the filly remained fascinated by something humans just couldn't see.

Her neck made the most graceful curve, Darby thought wistfully, and her golden mane wrapped around it in windblown strands, even though the morning was still.

"Are you ignoring me?" Darby asked.

Maybe Hoku was punishing her for separating her from Judge.

"Wow, anyone who doesn't think animals have feelings sure hasn't met you," Darby said with an incredulous laugh.

Hoku swiveled one ear in Darby's direction but stared toward Navigator and the buckskin.

"Hoku!" she called, and clapped her hands. For a minute she thought the sorrel had given in to her persistence, but no. Hoku pointedly swung her gaze past Darby and looked toward the Zink ranch and beyond.

Better bratty than terrified, Darby decided as Hoku gave a swish of her tail. She couldn't have said "go away" any more clearly if Darby were a bothersome fly.

"See you in a little while," Darby called, but she might as well have been talking to herself.

Darby counted her steps as she walked back toward Navigator. When she reached twelve, she sneaked a glance over her shoulder. Head high, the filly was watching Darby walk away.

"Caught you," Darby whispered, but Hoku whirled away so quickly, her mane swirled in a breeze of her own making.

Grinning, Darby crossed her fingers. Maybe everything would turn out all right.

As she approached, Kit pulled the front cinch snug and let down the stirrup he'd hooked up on Navigator's saddle horn. With relief, Darby realized this wasn't the day she'd learn to saddle.

"'Bout ready?" Kit asked.

"Sure," Darby said, and when Navigator snorted a hello, she moved in front of him and started to stroke his face.

"Don't pet that horse and don't stand in front of him," Jonah corrected her. "When you stand like that, dead in front of a horse and look him in the eye, you better want something from him."

"Sorry," Darby said. How could she have forgotten the no-petting rule overnight?

"Don't waste his attention," Jonah explained.

"I know," she said.

"You don't, but you will," he said, and the confidence in his voice kept Darby's feelings from being hurt.

"Ride out." He gestured off the bluff. "And look at each of our pastures. We have six. There's Sugar Mill and Upper Sugar Mill for the cattle, Two Sisters for the young horses — the one- to two-year-olds that we pretty much leave alone — Flatlands for the mares and foals, Pearl Pasture out near the forest — that's mostly two- and three-year-olds in training — Borderlands for the saddle herd and the stud compound. What are you doing?"

Darby froze in mid-reach for her notebook. "I was going to write that down. It's a lot to remember."

"You'll remember. Just ride out and look. By the end of the week, you'll know the names of all sixty horses on the place," Jonah said. "Start with the wet mares and foals."

Wet mares? Darby's mind sorted through her horse vocabulary and guessed they were the ones giving milk to their foals.

"Start with them?" Darby asked.

"Learn their names. Get to know them. Kit here, it only took him a couple days to learn 'em."

That made Kit a genius, Darby thought, but she only said, "I understand."

She watched Kit untie Navigator, back him up, then lead him toward the side hill where she'd mounted yesterday.

Excitement flashed through her, but she couldn't go to Navigator yet. Jonah hadn't finished giving orders.

"Look for Blue Ginger, Honolulu Lulu, Tail Afire—we call her Koko, but that's her registered name—Lady Wong, and Hula Girl."

"I really think I should write this down," Darby said, trying to keep the alarm out of her voice.

"It's just five names," Jonah said, "and their foals are—"

Nooo! Darby's brain wailed, but she concentrated.

"Blue Moon, a roan like his mom, Honolulu Half Moon—"

"Honolulu Lulu's baby?" Darby guessed.

"Right. She's a red sorrel with a matching mane. Then there's Moonfire, Black Cat, and Luna Dancer."

It was a good thing he didn't ask her to recite the names back, Darby thought. And she really hoped Navigator didn't feel like running or bucking this morning, because as soon as she got out of Jonah's sight, she *would* let go of the reins and write down all those names and colors.

"Questions?" Jonah asked, walking toward Navigator and Kit.

"Yes, a lot of them have Moon or Luna in their names. Why is that?"

"Our stud is Kanaka Luna. Luna, in Hawaiian, means—"

"Moon!" Darby finished for him.

"No."

Darby's blush embarrassed her as much as her mistake. But didn't luna have something to do with the moon? She'd read it a million times.

"In our language," Jonah said with a pointedness that, to Darby's surprise, included her, "it means *boss*, but we played off it to name his offspring."

Jonah gripped her shoulder and rocked it as if he could shake out the tension. "Loosen up. You just got here."

She smiled weakly. If he knew that, why did he expect so much?

As they walked side by side toward Navigator, the dark horse swung his head around to watch her with wise rust-circled eyes. She wanted to kiss him, but she didn't dare.

"And that sweatshirt?" Jonah said.

Darby looked down. It was faded and the pocket sagged from holding her book, but why did he care?

"What's wrong with it?" Darby asked.

"Nothing, but you need to decide whether to leave it here or wear it."

"Weather's mighty changeable here, just like home," Kit put in, glancing skyward.

Snarled white clouds streaked the Western sky, but she was riding in the opposite direction. Darby realized she was shifting from boot to boot. She needed more information to make all the decisions Jonah was forcing on her.

She made herself stand still and asked, "What do you think?"

"I think you'd be foolish to try to pull it off over your head while you're out riding all alone." Jonah nodded toward the open country. "You could fall off, and it's a long walk home."

 Chapter 10

Something black and bristly shoved through the underbrush on the hillside above the pasture of mares and foals.

Navigator had noticed it ten minutes ago. He didn't seem scared, just curious, stopping to gaze back at the spot every few strides.

Now the mares did the same. They left off grazing to cup their ears toward the rustling brush, alert for threats to their babies.

The black thing could be a big dog, Darby thought, but it moved with a bullying, out-of-my-way force that wasn't canine.

Sniffing with puzzlement, a chocolate-and-silver foal—maybe Moonfire?—set off to investigate the other creature. He'd only taken a few steps when his mother let him know the other animal was out-of-bounds.

The mare snorted. The foal ignored her.

She whinnied. He didn't stop.

Launching off strong haunches, the mare reached her foal in a single jump and gave him a nip. The foal squealed.

"That must be what they mean by 'tough love,' huh, boy?" Darby patted Navigator's neck to thank him for not acting up, but the gelding was busy watching the scolded foal work himself back into his mother's good graces.

Head hanging, the chocolate colt crowded against his mother's side, keeping her between him and the creature that had lured him away. After a few seconds of rubbing his head against the mare's flank, the colt began nursing, his little tail twisting from side to side as if he had to replace lost energy.

And neither of them holds a grudge, Darby thought. *People should be like that.*

Since the mares had everything under control, Darby rode toward the tree line.

So far, she'd followed all of Jonah's rules and the ride had been perfect.

While she was mounting, he'd said, "Don't be afraid. That horse isn't going to hurt you, so stay off his neck. Sit on your back pockets."

As she'd left the ranch yard, Darby had followed

Kit's directions to the least steep path off the bluff and
down to the pastures. She'd ridden past Sun House,
down the road Kimo had driven in on yesterday, and
turned right.

She'd sat straight, reins in her left hand, right
hand on her saddle horn, staying totally off
Navigator's neck, even when they were going downhill and she'd wanted to wrap her arms around him
and hide her face in his mane.

She didn't think she was afraid, but Jonah had
told her twice not to be, so she'd done a self-assess-
ment to see if she was kidding herself.

From head to toe, she'd checked her responses.

Was her brow sweating? No.

If her eyes were wide with terror, she couldn't feel
her eyelashes ticking back under her eyebrows.

Her hands weren't shaking and her knees weren't
knocking. Her teeth weren't chattering, either, or she
would have heard them.

I'm not scared, she'd thought, rearranging herself
to keep her back pockets in touch with the saddle,
and then, at the end of the slope, on level ground,
she'd glanced proudly back up toward the ranch.

Jonah had stood on the bluff, hands on his hips,
watching her.

He looked so forbidding, it probably wasn't possible, but she'd kind of wondered if he was the one
who was afraid.

Now, riding across the Flatland pasture, Darby

searched for a way into the woods that wouldn't involve gates.

Another of Jonah's rules was, If a gate is open, leave it open. If it was closed, leave it closed.

She understood why that was important, but she wasn't balanced enough to open and close a gate from horseback. And if she dismounted, could she open the gate, slip Navigator through, then close and lock the gate while holding the reins?

"Where are you going, boy?" Darby asked Navigator, then immediately imagined Jonah's voice saying, *Tell the horse where you want to go.*

They were headed downhill, and all the mares and foals flocked around them.

She studied the horses surrounding her. She loved feeling like part of their band, but she was unsure she'd gotten them matched to their names. Blue Ginger must be the blue roan with the tan foal. There was only one black foal. Logically, he must be Black Cat, and the elegant gray mare trailing him looked like she might be Lady Wong.

Darby wasn't sure which of the two brown mares was Honolulu Lulu and which was Hula Girl, but she'd bet Tail Afire was the fudge-brown horse with the silvery mane and tail, because Jonah had said she was nicknamed something like Cocoa.

"I should have worn my sweatshirt," Darby said out loud to Navigator.

She'd left her sweatshirt hanging in the tack

room, and though she wasn't really cold, the damp air saturated her T-shirt and jeans.

Dewy grass brushed Navigator's legs as they approached the forest pasture. Mist still hung among the trees.

At first, she saw no horses. Though she'd need a map to be certain, she thought Jonah had said Pearl Pasture, home to two- and three-year-olds, was the one bordering the forest.

A wooden gate was just ahead. How could she tell Navigator to position her so she could slide the bolt open, then relock it? That was a pretty complicated request.

"I might be able to make you understand," Darby told the gelding, "but what about them?" She nodded toward the mares and their foals.

The other horses might crowd through the open gate before she could lock it. They followed so closely that a bay colt with a half-moon on his forehead sucked on the cuff of her jeans while he walked beside Navigator. She couldn't risk having these youngsters slip into the next pasture with a bunch of rowdy two-year-olds.

But maybe she wasn't at Pearl Pasture at all, Darby thought. A wonderful flowery scent lingered on the air here, beckoning her to keep riding.

"Wouldn't you just love to explore that forest?" Darby asked, rubbing a strand of Navigator's coarse mane in her fingers. "But then, you probably already have."

Darby stood up in her stirrups to get a better view.

On the other side of the fence, she made out a trail so faint it might only have been a trick of the uncertain morning light. As her eyes traced it downhill into the forest, she heard the thump of hooves.

Five horses—a bay, a black, a roan, and two grays—cantered out of the forest.

"Oh, you beauties," Darby whispered.

The young horses didn't stop until they'd lined up with their chests against the fence. Their backs were wet. Dew hung in their manes and forelocks.

Navigator snorted a greeting. The mares backed away, swinging their muzzles against their foals. Darby couldn't blame the babies for their fascination. More horses emerged from the forest, including a palomino. He neighed, then struck at the ground over and over, until his hoof wore a rim of red mud.

Red mud. Darby wondered why the sight gave her chills.

Navigator pulled at the bit, ready to move on into the forest.

"Nope, no way," Darby told her mount. She glanced after the mares who moved their foals away at a trot. "I want to, boy, but it's only my second day."

So she needed to back away from the fence. But

she didn't know how. What twitch of the reins would tell Navigator what she wanted?

Steer the horse with your rein hand, like you would a car, Jonah had said, but she didn't know how to drive a car. And where was the reverse gear on a horse?

If she pulled back, she was telling him to stop. And he'd already done that.

With no other idea, she tried it anyway. Navigator's head flew up. His teeth hit the metal bit and his mouth gaped. Had she pulled hard enough to hurt him?

She moved her hand left, and he sidestepped left, still facing the fence. She moved her fist full of reins across in front of her, to the right. Navigator stamped and his ears flattened.

She couldn't blame him for being frustrated. She clearly wasn't using a language he understood.

"Try to guess what I want, boy," she begged the horse, then enunciated, "Back up."

But when she leaned away from his neck and increased the pressure on his bit, the gelding shifted his own weight back and jerked his front hooves into midair.

He was rearing like a wild stallion in a movie!

"No! That's not it!" Darby leaned forward.

Too bad about getting on his neck, she thought. She'd rather be a disgrace to the Kealoha dynasty of equestrians *in* the saddle, than *out* of it.

Finished showing her how inept she was, Navigator settled back on all four hooves.

Darby's hands were shaking. She couldn't do anything about that, but she eased upright in the saddle.

The gelding shook his head, then took a cautious step after the mares and foals.

"Yes! Good boy!" Darby encouraged, but as they moved away from the gate to Pearl Pasture, a warmth accompanied them. Darby had the odd feeling she wasn't leaving alone.

Darby gave the gelding a tiny tap with her heels.

Grumbling, Navigator moved on.

"Even I won't take back talk from a horse," she said, teasing the gelding, noticing her voice was higher than usual.

Navigator gave a loud sniff. He followed her cues to go up the Flatlands' only hill, but he did it at a trot.

Riding him at a walk on these steep hills was enough of a challenge for Darby, but Navigator ignored the gentle pressure on his bit and she was afraid to pull harder and cause another rear.

Would the hammering gait shake her out of the saddle? Her teeth clacked together and then, at the summit, Navigator's legs swung into a lope.

Setting her jaw with determination, Darby sat back in the saddle and clung to the saddle horn without dropping her reins. This gait was smoother than a trot, a glide-rock motion that let her fly with sun in her face, wind in her hair, and excitement fizzing through her veins.

All at once, Navigator swung his head left and dropped back to a trot, nearly jouncing her out of the saddle.

What did he see? Darby scanned the area with frantic eyes and spotted a huge bay horse with streaming mane, running straight at them.

Jonah's stallion. His name was—who knows? But it meant "boss," and the stallion's commanding approach convinced her he knew it.

The mares agreed. As if they were being herded, the mares, foals, and Navigator veered away from the fence. Was the stallion charging?

He's on the other side of the fence, Darby reminded herself.

The amazing bay stallion, all brown satin hide and sculpted muscles, wasn't gathering himself to jump.

"He's just getting a thrill from scaring us off," Darby told Navigator, but the gelding kept up his worried trot. She couldn't let Navigator get away with setting their pace.

And then she had it. She remembered reading something about riding a runaway to a standstill. She pulled her left hand toward her knee. The rein tightened and Navigator's nose followed. He turned in a circle for a few steps, then stopped.

It had worked! Of course, Navigator hadn't been a runaway. He'd barely been a trotaway. But she was satisfied.

"See? I know what I'm doing," she lied, but the horse's sulky walk told her he wasn't fooled. "Back there, by Pearl Pasture, where you had to rear to get my attention? I should have been able to figure out how to tell you what I wanted. I was just a little distracted."

Distracted wasn't really the word. Entranced was more like it.

At the gate to Pearl Pasture, a whiff of honeysuckle incense had coaxed her to come closer, to ride into the misty woods.

All at once, Darby knew why she'd longed to go down the jungle path.

Her dream! That path, those woods, even those horses were from her dream. If she'd passed through the gate and followed that trail, it might have taken her to the cottage in the jungle clearing. And maybe, this time, she would have discovered who or what stood behind that creaking door.

As she rode back toward Sun House, Darby stared through the frame of Navigator's dark ears and focused on the terrain ahead.

"I decide how we go home," she told the gelding.

He snorted, unimpressed.

Concentrate, Darby told herself. *Don't even think of looking back.*

And she didn't, because she had to be imagining the burning between her shoulder blades. It simply wasn't possible that she was being watched by hidden eyes.

Chapter 11

Darby had been riding for about ten minutes when she heard rapid hooves, and turned to see a rider following her.

It was Cade.

His poncho was such a dark green, it was almost black. He would have blended in with the rain forest if his horse hadn't been a gray splattered with black spots. His horse ignored the trail Navigator followed, lunging up the rocky face of the bluff, barely touching down between leaps.

Her first thought was that Cade was a careless rider set on breaking his horse's neck, but judging by the Appaloosa's eyes glittering amid his blowing black forelock, the horse was clearly having the time of his life.

"Hi—" Darby broke off, because she didn't want to break the horse's concentration.

Now the Appaloosa traversed the mountainside, coming her way.

Show-off, Darby thought, trying to summon up jealousy for Cade's riding skill. But she couldn't. He rode with a combination of spirit and ease, and Darby could only watch with wonder.

As he drew rein beside her, Cade gave the horse an openhanded pat on the neck, and the Appaloosa bobbed his head, asking for more.

While Cade lavished affection on his horse, Darby noticed Cade's saddle scabbard. He was just a kid, not much older than she was, but he carried a rifle.

A bedroll was tied on behind his saddle, and she smelled woodsmoke. Had he been camping? When Jonah sent someone out to check the fence, did he have to spend the night? Why hadn't he gone to school this morning with Megan?

Darby tried not to let her curiosity show.

Just in case he hadn't heard her before, she greeted him again.

"Hi."

"Hello." Cade touched his hat brim, but his smile looked forced, as if someone had ordered him to mind his manners.

Was he shy? Darby thought he was just critical.

Yesterday, he'd said Hoku might belong to a girl, but wasn't suitable for one.

Give me time, Darby thought. *I'll get good enough for her.*

Even now, Cade's eyes were on a fault-finding tour of the way she sat on Navigator. Instead of squirming, Darby made a comment of her own.

"Why do you wear a straw hat?" she asked. "When I was in Nevada, I heard a rancher say he wouldn't hire a cowboy who wore a straw hat because he'd spend all day chasing it."

Cade tilted his head back a little, peering out of the shade of his hat brim to meet her eyes.

"It's luahala, not straw, and it won't blow off because it was made to fit me." He glanced toward the vertical climb his horse had just bolted up.

"Yeah, I guess if it was going to blow off, that ride would've done it," Darby admitted. "What's luahala?"

"Leaves of the hala tree." Cade whipped the hat off and handed it to her. "A lady I know makes old-style paniolo hats."

He sounded proud, and as Darby took the hat and examined it, she could see why. The brown and beige weaving was intricate. It was a work of art, but that's not what struck her most.

Darby was shocked by how young Cade was. Fifteen, Jonah had said, but he looked even younger. Cade's hair was another surprise. Seeing his dark skin and brown eyes, she'd assumed he was

Hawaiian, but his hair was blond, parted in the middle and scraped back into—no, she wasn't imagining it—a short, tight braid.

Vaquero-style. Darby almost snapped her fingers in recognition.

An illustration in her fourth-grade California history textbook had shown a vaquero with hair just like Cade's. He'd held the reins of a prancing palomino, not a surefooted Appaloosa, but he'd worn a poncho like Cade's, too. And if her mom was right, paniolos had learned horsemanship from California vaqueros.

Didn't the kid realize he was a couple centuries late in copying his role models? Or maybe he didn't care. Either way, Darby felt a grudging admiration for him, except for his comment about Hoku not being a girl's horse.

Darby handed his hat back. As he put it on, he resumed his inspection of her saddle seat. She repositioned herself, sitting back in the saddle instead of leaning forward nervously.

"How's Navigator doin' for you?" he asked.

"He's being very tolerant." Darby rubbed the gelding's neck. "What's your horse's name?"

"Joker."

"Do you usually go to school with Megan?" Darby asked.

"No, Jonah's teaching me to paniolo, so I take correspondence classes."

"On the Internet?" Darby asked.

"No, I get a packet of lessons in the mail, do them, then mail 'em back."

Also like the old days, Darby thought. No nylon rope, but a braided leather one. No felt or straw hat, but one made of leaves. And he'd not only apprenticed himself to Jonah—a pretty medieval concept—but he handwrote his lessons and took them to the post office.

"I better get to work," he said. His horse had already moved off when he called over his shoulder, "Watch out for pigs when you're out there alone."

Watch out for pigs. Was he joking? What kind of tenderfoot did he take her for?

Shaking her head, Darby let Navigator follow Joker the rest of the way up the hill, then down the crushed black rock driveway into the ranch yard.

Sighting through Navigator's rust-tipped ears, she rode toward the hitch rail that stood midway between the tack shed and the house. As she did, Cathy came out of the office and fell into step beside the gelding.

"Jonah's talking with the farrier," Cathy whispered.

"Yeah?" Darby ransacked her brain for a reason why the presence of a farrier, a horseshoer, would make Cathy sound so secretive.

"Four horses have lost shoes in the last couple days, and they were only shod last week." Cathy took long steps to keep up with Navigator. "So he'll be giving the farrier a piece of his mind. That'll keep him occupied long enough for me to show you something."

An equine groan broke into their conversation. From her perch on Navigator, Darby spotted Hoku rolling in her grassy corral. So that's why she'd looked cleaner this morning.

Better yet, Hoku's sound was a groan of contentment, and she wouldn't put herself in such a vulnerable position if she wasn't settling in. Smiling, Darby decided to leave the filly undisturbed and see what Cathy had in mind.

After Darby slid clumsily to the ground, Cathy helped her tie up Navigator and said, "Come up and see our place."

Walking quickly, she led the way around the corner of the house, then up a white iron staircase that reminded Darby of a city fire escape.

"We'll have some tea."

"Great," Darby said.

"I don't suppose you ran into your *tutu* while you were riding?" Cathy asked.

"My what?"

"Great-grandmother. She lives—"

An explosion of barking erupted as Cathy opened the door. A dandelion puff of a dog darted at Darby's ankles and she jumped back.

"Did we disturb your nap?" Cathy scooped up the fluffy white dog Darby had seen patrolling the ranch with the big dogs. "The others are strictly outside dogs, but we make an exception for Pip, don't we?"

She nuzzled the dog. As Cathy drew back, its rose-petal tongue licked her. Then the dog squirmed free and hopped onto a low couch and burrowed into a pile of tropical print pillows.

Darby almost echoed the dog's comfy sigh.

The apartment felt like a tree house. Its only room was divided with fern-patterned screens and wicker furniture. Windows looked to the east, just like the lanai below.

"This is so cool," Darby said.

A collection of ukuleles were attached to a wall. Hula dancer dolls shared a shelf with flowerpots. Wind chimes made of shells tinkled in the breeze. There was no kitchen, but a jar of sun tea sat in one window.

The only thing that looked out of place was a desk shoved into a corner. Two round hatboxes were stacked on top.

Cathy paused in taking ice cubes from a bucket and dropping them into glasses. She tilted her head and asked, "Would you feel uncomfortable calling me *Aunty* Cathy?"

Startled, Darby thought about Cathy's question as she took the glass of tea. She studied the fingerprints she was making on the frosty glass and considered what to say. She couldn't think of a thing.

"It's a Hawaiian tradition," Cathy explained, with

a laugh. "One I like a lot. It's a way to show respect, but to me it feels like I'm more than a friend, though not quite family."

Darby settled into a rattan rocking chair and stole a quick glance up at Cathy. With her sun-streaked hair, open face, and kindness, she might make a pretty good aunt.

"So, we're not really related?" Darby asked.

"Not by blood," Cathy said, "but my husband Ben and his buddy Pani—"

"Kit's friend?" Darby interrupted, and Cathy nodded, but suddenly Darby realized that wasn't the important part of Cathy's sentence. *Her husband Ben,* she'd said. So, where was he?

"Together they worked on 'Iolani Ranch all through high school," Cathy went on. "Ben thought—and so did Jonah—they'd eventually run the ranch for him. Then Pani got it into his head that he'd go rodeoing."

Outside a high-pitched whinny sounded. Hoku didn't sound sad, but excited.

"Kit's bringing horses in. Your filly's just glad to see them," Cathy said, but then, for what seemed like a long time to Darby, Cathy ran her fingertip around the rim of her tea glass.

"Ben died in an accident fourteen months ago. You didn't know?" Cathy asked when Darby drew a loud breath. Then Cathy sighed. "Why on earth I expected Jonah to tell you—" She shook her head.

"He's hopeless when it comes to things like this, but I saw you riding up with Cade, and thought he might have mentioned it."

"No. I'm sorry," Darby mumbled.

"Did you hear that?" Cathy set down her glass suddenly.

"What?"

Cathy held out a hand to silence Darby and they both listened.

"I've just never heard Kit shout," Cathy said.

"I should go," Darby said, heading for the door. "Thank you."

"Go, but stay out of their—"

Darby was already out the door.

A quick glance to the right showed her six or seven horses moving up the path from the bluff. Kit rode behind on the buckskin, Biscuit. The cowboy slung his rope, moving the stragglers along, Darby guessed. Loose-limbed and easy in the saddle, Kit didn't look like he'd been shouting about anything bad.

But Hoku was plunging from fence to fence in her paddock.

Darby jogged toward her horse. She didn't run, because she didn't want to spook Hoku any more than the filly already seemed to be.

Two dark horses were trotting in the front of the group, ears pricked forward suspiciously, when a red bay flattened his ears and nipped the horse in front of him to move faster. The bay's victim jostled into a dun and then they were all running.

"Ffft!" Kit's warning to the horses was half-whistle, forced through his teeth, but it didn't slow them.

Darby skidded to a stop because she didn't want the horses to trample her, but she had to get to Hoku, to stand beside her and soothe her with civilized words, because Darby knew exactly what the filly was thinking. A herd was moving through the ranch. The filly wanted to join it.

Hoku galloped along the fence. With tilted head and searching eyes, she looked for a way out.

Survival depended on the herd. Hoku ran faster, pivoting in dust clouds each time she faced a barrier. Darby could feel her filly's panic.

Catch them! Don't let them leave you behind!

Hoku had remembered she was a mustang. Her instincts said escape, and she would—

There! The filly took aim and slammed her chest against the gate. It moved an inch and the wooden bolt jiggled in its slot. She'd found the weakest point in her enclosure.

As Hoku backed, then circled, away from the gate, Darby hoped the filly had learned her lesson. Crashing into the fence had hurt. Maybe she wouldn't do it again.

But the filly meant to try harder. She gathered herself on the far side of the paddock for a running start.

Darby darted ahead of the oncoming horses. She couldn't go inside Hoku's paddock, but she could tighten the bungee cord Kimo had looped around the gate.

Darby had almost reached the paddock gate when Hoku slammed into it again. The wooden bolt rattled. Hoku reared, forelegs scrabbling at the top of the wooden gate. Could she climb it?

No, Darby thought, but Hoku might die trying.

"Girl, get back!" Darby shouted. This time the filly's fragile trust worked against Darby. Hoku ignored her and attacked the gate again, making the bungee cord bounce.

I have to wind it tighter, Darby thought. If she leaned back with all her weight, she could stretch it, wind it at least once more above and below the bolt. It would hold. The only risky part would be unhooking it, but Hoku had circled to the other side of the paddock again.

Darby saw her chance. Her hands were in front of her, fingers reaching, touching, when power clamped around her waist and her boots left the dirt.

Jonah had come out of somewhere to swing her off her feet, away from the gate.

"No!" Darby shouted.

Her voice clashed and collided with the slam of the gate.

Jonah pulled Darby away, falling with her beneath him as Hoku burst through the gate.

Head pinned under Jonah's forearm, Darby twisted sideways to see Hoku's huge hooves at eye level. Then dust blinded Darby. The skittering hooves went quiet as Hoku launched herself up over them both with a leap. Darby held her breath in the long, silent instant before the filly cleared them, touched her hooves down on the other side, then galloped after the horses.

Chapter 12

Kit has a rope, Darby thought as she wrenched herself away from Jonah and they both struggled to their feet.

Kit was already swinging his rope when Hoku spotted him and forced her way through the band of saddle horses. In the seconds she took to decide on escape, Jonah ran for the gray horse he'd left ground-tied.

Darby had no idea how he got astride the gray. He seemed to fly, and the gray gelding pounced after Hoku.

Jonah leaned low on the gray's neck, trying to pass the filly. Was he trying to head her off?

The barbed-wire fence!

Darby's heart pounded as she ran after Hoku and

the two pursuing riders. Her horse was headed toward the Zinks' fields, which were fenced with barbed wire.

The filly had almost reached the boundary between the two ranches when Kit's arm flashed forward. His rope snaked out and encircled Hoku's neck.

Kit settled hard in the saddle and Biscuit tucked his hindquarters, practically sitting, but Hoku's struggle didn't stop.

Jonah maneuvered his gray in front of Hoku, but she didn't shy away. The filly gave a groan that Darby heard over her pounding feet. Hoku's head whipped back. Her muzzle pointed at the sky. Then, with all the strength in her neck and shoulders, the filly gave a mighty heave and flung herself at the fence post to Jonah's left.

Hoku was dragging Biscuit! The buckskin's hooves plowed grooves in the dirt as he skidded behind her.

Kit gave a startled shout as Hoku tried to jump. When she couldn't tow the buckskin up and over, the filly faltered. Her golden forelegs hit the top wire. It was pain that finally pierced her desire to escape.

Hoku screamed.

But that wasn't the most horrible sound. Twangs like breaking guitar strings came an instant before the fence post cracked and Hoku went down in a tangle of wire.

Jonah was off his horse, holding something in his hand.

Not a gun! Darby thought wildly, and it wasn't.

Her grandfather clutched wire cutters, but Hoku's legs flailed to break away from the twisted metal prongs. Each time Jonah had to duck away, Hoku snared herself more tightly.

The filly's head and neck thrashed weakly as she tried to roll upright. Her legs were no help to her. Caught and kicking, Hoku strained in a bloody battle to break free.

At last Kit knelt beside the filly, grabbed the cheek piece of her halter, and used both hands to force her head toward the ground. Teeth bared, Hoku tried to reach him.

"Stay down, poor girl," Darby moaned. Her ankles almost gave way as she crouched next to Kit and crooned to Hoku. "It's okay, girl. You'll be fine. Hoku, let us help you, oh, please."

The filly quit fighting. Hoku's nostrils flared open and red, and her wide eyes locked on Darby's.

You, too? the mustang seemed to accuse, but then her neck wobbled and Kit pressed the filly's head flat against the ground.

Hoku's breath blew loudly. Dirt stuck to her wet lips, and finally her eyes closed.

Jonah swarmed around the filly's legs, clipping, cutting, cursing. Finally, he peeled back lengths of wire and exhaled.

"What's her hide made of, Kevlar?" Jonah's words came out in amazement.

Kevlar. Wasn't that what they made bulletproof vests from? Darby stared at Jonah, trying to decipher what he meant. His hands were bloody, but he looked down at Hoku, blinking.

"A couple scratches on her knees is all."

"No," Kit whispered in disbelief.

Jonah held out a hand, presenting the filly as evidence.

Loosening his grip and stroking the sorrel's neck, Kit peered at her legs.

"Warm water and salve will take care of that," he told Darby.

Relief rushed through her. The wire hadn't cut through flesh down to the tendons. No injuries would keep Hoku from running headlong into the wind.

Darby closed her eyes and saw green and blue comets of light behind her lids. She smelled the crushed grass beneath Hoku and heard Jonah's gray horse and the buckskin dragging their reins as they ignored the commotion and looked for something to eat.

Everything is okay, Darby thought, until she opened her eyes and saw Kit's frown.

"What?" Darby demanded.

"Let's watch her get up. Her neck's hot here." Kit touched Hoku's sweating neck with the back of his right hand. "Burnin' up."

Why wouldn't it be hot? Darby wondered. Hoku had

used her chest as a battering ram, then run a mile across the fields, only to end in a spiked spiral of wire.

"She pulled Biscuit after her," Kit told Jonah.

Darby remembered the grooves cut in the dirt as the little mustang had dragged the buckskin.

"Get her up," Jonah ordered.

"Can't she rest?" Darby asked him.

Now that the filly was quiet at last, Jonah couldn't wait to disturb her. And this was all his fault. If he'd let Darby tighten that bungee cord, Hoku might still be in the corral.

Darby ignored the logical part of her mind that insisted she couldn't have moved fast enough to do what she'd planned. She was sick of logic.

"She'll rest after we get her home." Jonah stepped around the filly, took the rope from Kit, and flicked the end of it at Hoku's back.

"How can you—?"

"I want that cursed wild blood to get moving to her muscles," Jonah snapped.

Kit still squatted next to Darby. He faced her to explain, "If she's pulled something in her neck or anywhere else, we need to encourage circulation."

As Kit stood, so did Darby, but Hoku didn't move.

"C'mon, crazy horse," Jonah barked, "on your feet."

This time his hand rose up and down, flipping the rope that led to the loop on her neck. Hoku's eyelids sprang open.

Left arm held tight to his side, Kit swung into the saddle, rode Biscuit off a few feet, then looked back at the filly.

Hoku gave a guttural sound, begging the buckskin to stay with her.

"She hurts," Darby told her grandfather. "Shouldn't we call the vet?"

"I'm not throwing good money after bad," Jonah said.

Darby smothered the flare of her temper. This was no time to battle her grandfather, so she tried again. "But she can't get up."

"She'd better," Jonah said. "A horse who can't move won't get well. Her circulation will go, then her digestion, then the whole horse shuts down."

Though the words were harsh, they were true.

Hoku had to get up and move around. Darby couldn't allow the golden filly to lay here for days, pining for her herd and home, not rising to eat or drink, until she simply gave up.

Do something, Darby told herself. *Push her. Coax her. Don't just stand here, staring down at Hoku as if you can't move, either.*

"Darby, go over, tie Kona's reins out of the way, and give him a smack on the rear. Get him to follow Kit," Jonah said, and his voice was kinder than before. "Hoku'll go with them, I bet."

She might have been sleepwalking as she moved toward the big dappled-gray Quarter Horse and did as Jonah said. Kona barely felt her slap, but Jonah clucked to the horse and he jogged after Biscuit.

Hoku's legs thrashed, but she didn't rise.

"Come around on this side." Jonah gestured Darby over to his position, about five feet behind the prone Hoku. "We might have to help her."

"Is she going to be okay?" Darby asked.

Hearing Darby's voice, Hoku's eyes rolled white in an attempt to see behind her, where Darby stood.

Darby moved closer.

"The cuts on her forelegs are superficial," Jonah said, but that wasn't much of an answer, and her grandfather frowned as he went on.

"Her neck, I think, is strained pretty badly. She's young, weakened by the voyage, without the muscles to do what she tried to do. A bad neck can be trouble, since a horse, wanting to stand, swings his head for the momentum, then rolls toward his belly and scrambles around with his legs to get up.

"You've seen movies of cheetahs running? Or a housecat walking on the back of a couch? Both use their tails for balance. That's not how it is with a horse. Even with those big hindquarters, she uses her head and neck for balance."

Darby moved closer to Hoku, and when Jonah didn't reprimand her, she crouched by the filly's neck. With her left hand, she moved clumps of mane aside. Her right hand smoothed over the white hair from the freeze brand on Hoku's neck.

At last, Darby was touching her horse again, but she did it softly, as if she were trying not to disturb the surface of water.

"Good," Jonah said. "Now, her neck bones make kind of an *S* shape under the hair, hide, and muscles. See if you feel anything like a vertebra out of whack."

Darby glanced up desperately. "How would I know?"

"Just see if she'll let you feel around. I'm pretty sure it's a muscle problem, not bone."

Concentrating all her intelligence into her fingers, Darby tried. She felt a long, warm place, probably the strained muscle Kit had noticed, but nothing else. And yet the filly didn't try to go after the other horses. In fact, she emitted a huge sigh that rushed through her body and made Darby look up at Jonah again.

"She's relaxing when you touch her," he said. "Massage might work with her. Some trainers swear by it."

Kona picked that moment to pause, nearly back to the paddock, and neigh for Hoku to follow.

The sorrel's legs churned. Jonah bent to give her back a push and motioned Darby around front.

"Start walking," he said.

"But—" She wasn't about to leave her horse behind.

"Go," he muttered, and as Darby took a hesitant step, Jonah placed both palms against Hoku's back and rocked her, giving the filly the momentum she needed to roll onto all four hooves and stand.

Head hanging from her strained neck, nose almost touching the grass, Hoku focused on Darby's feet. She risked one step, then another. Stopping only to blow dust from her nostrils, the filly followed Darby all the way back to the paddock.

When Darby paused, Jonah said, "Don't stop here."

"Fine," Darby said under her breath. She'd given up protesting, because Jonah just kept making sense.

She was surprised when he slipped the end of Kit's rope into her hand.

"Follow me," he told her, "but don't pull if she stops. If she's ever going to be of use, you've got to baby that neck."

Darby and Hoku followed Jonah past the paddock, downhill, on by the tack shed and Kit's house. They passed a chicken coop and a rooster crowed their approach to his hens, which only scratched and fluttered, hardly noticing.

A hawk swooped overhead, followed by smaller birds.

Where were they going? Darby wondered.

Quiet closed in around them as they walked a dirt track that meandered near the bluff. On her right, Darby saw a jumble of grayed-wood cages. They looked old, and sat in such deep shade, Darby couldn't tell what they'd been built to hold.

Finally, they came to a round pen with high sides. Made of wood that smelled freshly cut, it was probably the newest structure on the ranch.

Last night when she'd been thinking that there had to be somewhere on the ranch that she could be alone with Hoku, she'd pictured something like this.

Darby glanced back at the filly. Her shuffling steps were the opposite of this morning's fierce grace. Darby's heart hurt. She never should have wished for a second chance to bond with Hoku.

"Don't like this corral. I want a horse to be able to see out, but for her, for now, this might be safer. Walk her on in," Jonah said.

At the sound of the opening gate, Hoku stopped. Her head didn't jerk up, but her ears pointed forward.

"You're hurt, but you still don't want to be locked up, do you, baby?" Darby asked as Hoku stepped gingerly after her.

"Now," Jonah said, "take a hard look at Kit's loop. Study it. Then, as carefully as you ever moved in your life, widen it until you can slip it off over her ears."

"But she's so head-shy," Darby whispered.

"We can't fix that now. Just don't let her even think of jerking back."

Hands shaking and drained of energy, Darby told herself she could keep going for a few more minutes. She concentrated on the loop, and pushed thoughts of spinal injuries from her mind. She hoped a mistake wouldn't paralyze her filly.

"My pretty girl. I'll never hurt you." Darby cooed to Hoku, hoping the filly would concentrate on her voice as she had on that awful day in the snow.

With delicate fingers, Darby pulled the rope until it slid smoothly, making the loop bigger. Her hands didn't waver a millimeter. She lifted the rope off without touching the filly's neck, ears, or a single whisker on her chin.

"Without turning your back on her, hand it to me," Jonah said.

It seemed pretty ridiculous that Jonah was still afraid for her to turn her back on Hoku, but she went along with his request. Reaching behind her, Darby extended the rope and felt him take it.

She sighed. Almost done.

"Kit's coming up here with hot water and antibiotic salve. You'll clean and doctor her cut legs," Jonah said.

"But I—"

"We'll stand here and talk you through it, and be here in case she turns on you."

In case she turns on you. They weren't comforting words, but Darby looked down as she felt something move against her ankle.

Because her strained neck forced her to keep her head lowered, Hoku was checking out the world at hoof level. She sniffed the hem of Darby's jeans, where the colt had nibbled it this morning. Darby's weariness fell away and she smiled. The filly was injured and scared, but still curious about the world around her. That had to be good, didn't it?

Just then, Hoku gave Darby's jeans a tender lick. Wow, she'd never known horses licked anything but salt blocks. What did it mean?

Without moving the rest of her body, Darby turned her gaze toward her grandfather.

Nodding, he said, "This might not have been the worst thing that could have happened. If your filly's not ruined, I think you've got yourself a second chance."

Chapter 13

Darby had spent an hour sitting with her back against the fence, watching Hoku try to understand what had happened to her, when Jonah called her out of the pen.

At first she didn't want to go.

"Let her doze while you go over to the office," Jonah urged her. "Cathy made ham and cheese sandwiches for lunch. You can eat while you read your fax."

"A fax for me?" Darby asked.

"From your friend in Nevada," Jonah said. "What surprises you? That there are fax machines in Nevada or in Hawaii?"

"That anyone would send *me* a fax," Darby said.

"Well, someone did. Samantha Forster. She's the one who knows wild horses, right?"

Darby nodded, her pulse beating like crazy at her wrists.

Sam must have learned something about Hoku's past. And she'd notified her by fax? Darby amended her first thought. Sam must have learned something *important* about Hoku.

Darby almost blurted her thoughts to Jonah, since he'd wanted to know more about the filly's background and bloodlines, but she waited, just in case the news wasn't as exciting as she was imagining.

They walked toward the office together. Darby assumed Jonah would have lunch with her, until he headed for the hitching rack and untied Kona.

"Aren't you eating?"

"Later, maybe."

Kit walked out of the office as Darby started in. First he touched the brim on his black cowboy hat, as if he planned to keep walking, then he stopped.

"Sorry about hurting your horse," he apologized. "I've seen steers pull the way she did, but never a little filly."

For the first time since the accident, tears stung Darby's eyes. It didn't matter that Hoku was young, delicately made, and a filly. Her heart was wild.

"It wasn't your fault," Darby said, blinking before Kit saw her tears and felt even worse. "If you hadn't roped her, who knows where she'd be."

Kit cleared his throat. "Thanks," he said, then looked after Jonah. "He going to get Luna?"

Darby shrugged.

"The farrier's on his way, and I was supposed to bring the stud up after I brought the saddle horses."

"Since Hoku got loose—" Darby was about to say, *I think he'll understand,* but she reminded herself she was talking about Jonah. There was as great a chance he wouldn't see why Kit hadn't gone back for Luna, as the chance that he would.

"She has spirit. I'll give her that," Kit said, glancing in the direction of the round pen.

"I know it!" Darby said, feeling giddy at the compliment.

"But after all she's been through, don't get your hopes up too high. A lot can happen after horses are injured. They go off their feed, develop infections, and they can settle into depression, just like people."

It was only when Kit's eyes dropped to her hand that Darby realized she'd covered her heart. She let her hand fall to her side.

"Still, if you can keep her up and moving around, help her eat and drink, and give her something to live for," Kit said with a grin, "you just might have yourself a horse."

Head spinning with hope, despair, and a longing for her mother, Darby wandered into the coolness of the office.

Cade sat astride a chair, turned backward to face

Cathy's desk. Kimo stood beside him, holding a sand-wich in one hand and a sheet of paper in the other.

"We were just talking about your horse," Cade said.

"You may not know this, having grown up in the city"—Cathy nodded toward Kimo, though she spoke to Darby—"but a ranch is like a family. Every-one lives close together and thinks your personal stuff is meant to be shared."

"I'll remember that," Darby said, snatching the faint, close-spaced sheet from Kimo.

"That's gonna help a lot," he said, looking totally unashamed as he nodded at the fax.

Darby was so eager to read Sam's message, she didn't even pretend to be mad. Instead, she told Cathy, "You can read over my shoulder if you want."

Dear Darby,
YOUR HORSE IS THE PHANTOM'S LITTLE
SISTER!!! Brynna said it was too early to call, but
I told her I had to tell you RIGHT NOW, so she let
me use the fax machine she got for her new job.

Jen and I would make good spies! We found out
your horse is two and a half years old. Her dam is
Princess Kitty, a running Quarter Horse, and her
sire was Smoke, a gray mustang my dad used for
working cattle.

Ha! Darby looked up from the letter, feeling vin-dicated. Jonah raised Quarter Horses and thought they were the crowning touch on the entire equine species. Now, who was a range rat!

Kitty lived on River Bend Ranch until she went to Jen's family. She was in foal to Smoke, but lost that baby and so she was bred back to Smoke and foaled at about the time the Kenworthys had to sell their ranch to Linc (the jailbird) Slocum. Your filly was sold as a weanling to a local rancher, but he lost his place, too (I hope ranching is easier in Hawaii!) and sold all his horses to Shan Stonerow.

Darby caught her breath. Did that mean Hoku wasn't wild? That BLM had made a mistake branding her? And worse, allowing her to be adopted?

Darby only worried for a second. What were the odds the man would come to Hawaii and demand they return his horse? She read on.

I've never met Shan Stonerow. Neither has Jen. But he has a rep. for breaking horses "fast and dirty." He's famous for teaching them who's boss with a long quirt—

As Darby's finger hovered over the word, trying to remember what it was, Cathy said, "It's a whip. Usually it goes around the wrist and it has long strands of leather."

Darby was sure everyone could hear her swallow

as she imagined the quirt's link with Hoku's head-shyness.

> —and we heard he actually saddled your horse as a yearling! He tried to sell her to our friend Katie Sterling by saying she needed a female rider because she hated men. Who could blame her after his "training"?

If Cade caught her guilty glance, he didn't show it, but Darby cautioned herself against jumping to conclusions. She'd convinced herself Hoku disliked Cade, when she apparently didn't like *any* men.

> We put Shan's phone number at the bottom of this fax. You could call him if you want to see how your filly ended up wild or find out how long she was on the range. Kit (tell him we said HI!) knows about Shan. His (Kit's) grandfather says Shan turns out horses he can't sell—"throwing away things of value" is how he put it—on tribal lands. But Clara from the café says Shan told her the filly could escape from a locked closet! So who knows how she turned wild?
> What we couldn't find out is if she's related to Yellow Tail. She looks like him, but no way did a filly fight the Phantom. I saw that battle with my own eyes!

I hope you're having fun in Hawaii. Please hug the Phantom's little sis for me!

Samantha Forster

Darby had just finished reading when Kit stuck his head back in the office.

"Cathy? Could you find our last feed store bill? Seems to me we got shorted a sack of grain," Kit said. "I'd look for it myself, but I'm keeping an eye on the farrier. He's not too pleased about waiting for Luna and I don't want him to take off."

"I'm on it," Cathy told him, then made a shooing motion. "Just as soon as everyone clears out of my office. Darby, don't forget to take your sandwich."

When they stepped outside, Kimo went to clean the paddock Hoku had been in. As Kit turned to go back to the horseshoer, Darby rushed after him.

"Could you look at this?" Darby asked Kit.

"Later. I've got to get back over there," he said, glancing toward the farrier's truck.

"Please," she begged.

Kit took the fax and read as he walked.

Darby could still smell the horse salve on her hands as she ate her sandwich. She should wash them now, but she was too busy watching Kit's expression change as he read.

After a few strides, Kit stopped, looked up, and rubbed the back of his neck.

"So, she's got decent bloodlines, but she's been beaten, pushed too fast, then she taught herself to run away. And we let her practice that again today. Doesn't sound like she'll be any trouble at all." Kit returned the letter and walked away.

Mystified, Darby turned to Cade. She meant to ask him if Kit was joking or being sarcastic. Instead, she thought of yesterday and the blood blooming on his shirt.

"Hoku didn't hurt you too much, did she?"

"Why do you want to know?" Cade asked with a suspicious frown.

"Because I'm going to be working with her, and I'm not very experienced—" Darby broke off. She deserved a medal for the understatement of the year.

"Okay," Cade said. He tugged at the neck of his loose linen shirt, using both hands to pull it down far enough that Darby saw a mottled maroon hoof mark, stamped on the skin over his breastbone.

Darby knew she winced, but she didn't dish out sympathy, since he didn't seem to want it.

"Just be careful," he said, squaring the shirt back on his shoulders.

"No, really?" Darby snapped, then covered her mouth.

Cade didn't deserve her sarcasm, but she was worried about Hoku, and scared for herself. Most of all, she wondered what it was about living on a ranch that caused people to avoid medical care.

No vet for Hoku. No doctor for Cade. An injury like that should have sent him to the emergency room. Instead, he'd gone out to hammer fences and sleep on the ground.

Of course she'd be careful. She wasn't tough enough to survive the consequences of being brave!

"I'm not saying she'll hurt you, but since she's been beaten . . ." Cade blew air into his cheeks, then slowly released it. "She might do it and not mean to, you know?"

Darby shook her head. "I'm not trying to be dense, but I don't understand what you're saying."

Cade rubbed the right side of his jaw for such a long time, Darby noticed it jutted slightly to one side, as if it had been broken.

"Kind treatment won't erase her memory. Before I lived here, my stepdad never minded giving me a pop when he thought I deserved one." He touched his jaw again. Darby had the feeling Cade's jaw hadn't always looked like it did now. "That hasn't happened again, not since Jonah, uh, *talked* to my dad. . . ." A fleeting smile crossed Cade's face. "But since you can't tell Hoku she's safe, you've got to show her. In a while she might believe you, but even then she won't forget."

Darby was still groping for something to say when Cade walked off. Anyone would have been uneasy after such a confession, but most people would have said *something*. Even, "Gee, that's too bad," would have been better than standing there gulping.

Still kicking herself for acting like an insensitive jerk, Darby had started back toward Hoku's new corral when Jonah rode up on Kona, his gray, leading Luna. The stallion pranced at the end of his lead rope, showing off for Hoku. His bay neck had the shape and tension of a bow, Darby thought, drawn so tight it trembled.

"Darby, come help me with this stud."

Is he serious? Darby asked herself.

She followed alongside, trying to read Jonah's face.

"Luna challenges new people," he said, as if that explained his request.

"Like me?" Darby asked, remembering how the bay stallion had charged the fence when she'd been out on Navigator.

"Like the farrier," Jonah said, as if she weren't very smart. "Meet me up there. You might learn something."

Both horses trotted, and she couldn't keep up. Before she reached the tack shed where the farrier, a balding man in a leather apron, stood with his hands on his hips, Darby heard Luna make a squalling sound.

No, it wasn't a squall. Darby had never heard

such a sound, and she had a feeling it was peculiar to disgruntled stallions. Raspy and low, it was sort of a cross between a lion and an eagle. Each time the farrier took a step closer, Luna lashed out with his hind hooves.

Jonah didn't say a word to the horse, just suddenly moved in.

"It's all about space," Jonah said to Darby. "I'm taking his."

Jonah slipped his hand around the cheek piece of the stallion's halter. Jonah didn't pull or jerk—just held on.

With one toss of his head, the mighty bay could have lifted her grandfather off his feet. He didn't.

"It's *mana* versus *mana*, my spirit testing his," Jonah said, and yet he just stood there.

When the stallion's eyes rolled toward Jonah, her grandfather stepped closer. Finally, Jonah and the stallion stood shoulder to shoulder.

Snorting, the stallion's brown eye fixed on Jonah's. Then, as if he actually believed Jonah was the stronger animal, Luna lowered his head and blew through his lips.

Without a fight, he'd agreed to let Jonah take charge.

The magic touch, Darby thought.

Sam and Mrs. Allen had insisted Darby had it, but she'd done nothing like that.

She hadn't stared down a huge stallion. She'd only taken pity on a fallen filly and stayed with her. Sure, Hoku had welcomed her and, yeah, it *was* pretty unusual to lay in the snow and tell her stories, but it wasn't what Jonah had just shown her.

"Okay," Jonah said, nodding to tell the farrier he could go ahead and shoe Luna.

Cautiously, the man moved in, but Darby looked down at her hands, hoping they contained some of Jonah's ability to communicate with horses.

"Go get carrots from in there, two or three, and feed him until you're sure he's settled down," Jonah told Darby.

Kit tilted his head toward the tack room, hinting where the carrots were kept.

Better do the task instead of mulling over your superpowers, Darby said mockingly to herself. She went into the dim tack room. Squinting, she saw shelves of horse medicine, hardware, a coffee cup that smelled like it wasn't empty, and a bunch of saddles and bridles, but no carrots.

Oh sure, she thought, *give the new kid another impossible task.* But part of her didn't care. She couldn't stop wondering if she'd inherited something special from Jonah.

She spotted the plastic bag of carrots, snatched two in each hand, and rejoined the men outside.

The stallion bumped her hand and grabbed a carrot before she offered it to him.

She broke another carrot and balanced half on her flattened palm. The stallion's teeth grazed her hand. He had no interest in biting, but as he crunched the carrot, he didn't mind drizzling her with juice.

The look in his eye told Darby exactly what he thought of her.

Impostor, Luna said with a snort.

Maybe I'm an amateur, Darby thought, *but I'm no phony.*

Everyone had to begin somewhere, and she'd already made a start. She couldn't wait to get back to Hoku.

Chapter 14

When Darby walked the path back to Hoku, Jonah came with her. He brought a brimming bucket of water and Darby carried a kit of grooming tools.

Hoku's fluting sound of recognition, higher than a nicker, squeezed Darby's heart.

She knows my footsteps, Darby thought. She glanced at Jonah to see if he'd noticed, but he was pointing out the jumble of old wooden cages Darby had seen before.

"My dad had a lot of moneymaking schemes," Jonah told her. "Ran a piggery, which was pretty successful, but these cages were for the foxes."

"He raised foxes?" Darby asked. "What for?"

"Fur coats," Jonah said.

Darby shuddered. She hated the idea of killing animals for something so frivolous, and the logical side of her mind wondered if it didn't make more sense to raise fur animals in a cold climate.

"That venture went bust quick," Jonah said, "and he barely dodged an arrest for smuggling."

Every time she learned more about her extended family, Darby wondered how her mom had kept them secret.

Darby sneaked a sideways look at Jonah. She longed to hear his explanation of that letter to her mom. And she wanted to meet the great-grandmother who lived, apparently hidden, on this ranch. Since Jonah had brought up family matters, was this a good time to start prying?

"She's kept her appetite," Jonah observed as soon as Hoku came into sight.

The filly had been standing with her forelegs spread wide apart to nibble grass without flexing her strained neck.

"Think of being a prey animal, stuck like that," Darby said. She hadn't really meant to say the words aloud.

"She wouldn't make it in the wild," Jonah said.

"Wouldn't she?" Darby asked. She didn't mean to be defiant, but she'd just been thinking about Hawaiian predators. She didn't think a mongoose could bring down a horse. "What could get wild horses here?"

Jonah made a sound of disgust, but he didn't answer.

Darby heard snuffling and looked up to see that Hoku had tottered unsteadily to their side of the pen. Nose low to the ground, she tried to see through the close-set boards.

"Slip in there. She'll be nervous since she can't hold her head up and watch everything around her. She needs to know where you are every second. Talk to her and don't stop," Jonah said as he unlocked the gate.

A lurch of excitement made Darby swallow hard. She was going into Hoku's new realm, alone.

"I'm coming in, girl," Darby said.

"Take a brush," Jonah told her as he held the gate.

She did, and then he closed her inside with Hoku.

Feeling self-conscious in front of him, she asked, "What should I say to her?"

"Anything. It doesn't matter."

Darby hesitated. Even though Hoku wouldn't understand, maybe she'd mention something about grooming to explain the brush she carried.

"You look a little frowzy, girl," Darby said.

Did Jonah laugh?

No matter. The filly's ears stood upright as a unicorn's horn, listening to her.

"Your cruise didn't do much for your hair. It looks less like candlelight satin and more like—" Darby paused. Straw was the first thing that came to mind, but that wasn't it. "Like this girl who was at my old school? Her hair was always a different color, and I'm sad to say, pretty horse, that your mane looks like her bleached-blond stage."

Hoku's muscles went taut. She tried to lift her head, then squealed in pain.

"It's okay," Darby said, but Hoku backed away, as if she knew Darby planned to touch her. She looked back at Jonah. "Maybe I'm rushing her."

"No. Remember what you said about being prey? If she was in the wild, she'd have the stallion, the lead mare, and plenty of other horses to be on the lookout for trouble. Keep your eyes on her and don't go anywhere near her head."

Darby thought of Shan Stonerow and the quirt again. If he'd slashed her in the face with it . . . She cut off her violent thoughts by continuing her one-sided conversation with Hoku.

"I think you just need to be reminded how much you liked this at Mrs. Allen's ranch," Darby told Hoku as she followed her around the pen.

"That's it," Darby said when Hoku let her get within reach.

Darby made a gentle dab with a brush at the sorrel's shoulder. Hoku took two steps away, then stopped. Darby followed the filly around the corral and didn't get within reach again.

Jonah swished the bucket outside the pen and

Hoku uttered a thirsty nicker.

"Try her with this," he said.

When Jonah opened the gate and handed Darby the bucket, Hoku skittered out of reach, almost falling. But the filly was thirsty and she returned to drink.

Her brown eyes showed over the bucket's rim. Wary, she wouldn't let anything sneak up on her.

"Work your way up to her neck," Jonah instructed. "If it's just a pulled muscle, massage might get some blood in there to start healing."

Darby raised the brush, about to begin, when Jonah added, "Be careful. It's gonna be tender."

Hot and frustrated by the way Hoku kept moving away from the brush, Darby stopped and rubbed at her nose. This pen had probably had a dirt floor when it was built, but daily rains had brought grass creeping back. She wondered if it was the dirt, grass, or something in the air that made her lungs labor.

"Forget the brush. Use your hand like she let you before," Jonah said.

It worked. Darby smiled as her fingers touched Hoku's back, her mane, and then moved *under* the pale mane to touch the filly's neck. Hoku stiffened, but she didn't move away.

Darby curled her fingers in light strokes, moving from just above the strained muscles, down to the filly's withers. She made little circles sometimes, but mostly just short, straight lines, like she thought horses' teeth would make when they groomed each other. Each time she started over again, she used a bit more pressure.

Hoku stayed still. In fact, when Darby looked down, she saw the filly's golden eyelashes closed and unmoving.

How long would she have to wait before leaving the filly? It would only take five minutes to run to her room and get her asthma medicine, and it was still early enough to head off real breathing trouble.

"I've got work to do," Jonah said. "Come on out, but sit here with her."

Darby did. She sat with her horse for hours, listening to Kimo hammering as he fixed the Zinks' fence and ignoring the tightness in her chest. As she watched Hoku sleep, the little oxygen-carrying branches in Darby's lungs unfurled, and gradually breathing grew easy.

A dark curtain of rain hung high in the sky and each time Darby looked, the gray had sneaked a bit lower.

Soon, she supposed, rain would actually fall, but now it was only humid, or "muggy" as her mom would say, and the orange T-shirt kept her plenty warm.

After a quick dinner, Darby asked Jonah if she could spend the night with Hoku.

"I'll go upstairs and get a blanket off my bed," Darby suggested. "If Mom calls—"

Jonah pulled a cell phone from his pocket and handed it to her. "I'll have her call you down here," he said. "Go ahead to her pen." Then, just when Darby thought he was transforming into one of those nice storybook grandfathers, Jonah added, "While you're alone, don't go inside the corral with that horse or you'll manage to get yourself hurt."

"I won't," she said.

"Not under *any* circumstances, or you're on the next plane home."

"I promise," she said.

An hour later, Darby took down her ponytail, rumpled her hair in relief, and arranged the sleeping bag Jonah had unrolled for her.

Before he left them alone, Jonah insisted Darby try to get Hoku to taste some oats. The filly wasn't interested.

He had Darby feel the skin around Hoku's knees for infection, too.

"Do they feel swollen? Warm? Be sure now," he said.

So much depended on her answer, Darby closed her eyes as she put a palm on Hoku's back legs, then tried to remember the exact degree of heat as she set her palm over the filly's wire-cut knees.

"They feel the same temperature," she said.

Jonah nodded, then gestured for her to come out. He tested the bolt on the corral gate, then started to walk away.

Darby lowered herself to sit cross-legged on her sleeping bag.

As she looked after Jonah, she wished he'd glance over his shoulder and say something like, "If you need anything, feel free to wake me up," or "Do you want me to stay and help you keep watch?", but he didn't.

"Hey!" Darby shouted, though she knew instantly that it was a rude way to catch her grandfather's attention.

He turned, but she couldn't think of anything to say.

He looked tired, she thought. After all, he was pretty old, and he'd lifted her off her feet by Hoku's corral, and rolled them both out of the way of the filly's hooves. Then he'd ripped up his hands cutting Hoku free of the barbed wire.

Now, he started walking back toward her.

I'm so dumb, Darby thought.

"Yes?" Jonah asked, and since he didn't sound grumpy, she managed to come up with a question.

"Are there any night-prowling animals I should know about?"

Jonah drew a breath and looked into the starry sky. Probably he was wondering why, since he already had one foster child, Cade, he'd taken her on. Or maybe, Darby thought, crossing her fingers, Jonah was just thinking deeply.

"There's the *menehune*," he said.

"Many-who-knee?" Darby repeated.

"The little people, but they won't bother you, and the horses won't wander up from the pasture and down the road this far. Even after all these years, they don't like the fox smell," Jonah said.

He shoved his hands in his pockets, waiting for her to release him.

"Okay, thanks," Darby said. Trust her grandfather to mix fact and fiction and let her sort it out.

He rocked back on his bootheels and snapped his fingers silently. "You know, you really might hear owls, but they're our family *'aumakua.*"

Darby didn't even try to mimic the word, but she recognized it. In the letter to her mom, he'd said, "I am grateful for the chance to teach her of her family, her 'aumakua . . .'"

"They're our family's guardians," Jonah explained. "Sometimes they advise us through dreams and sometimes they show up as protectors."

Darby could believe owls lived around here, with all the trees to perch in and fields where mice could be plucked up and swallowed for dinner. But how could an owl guard a human?

"Is that why one's painted on the trucks?" she asked. "Because they guard us?"

Jonah nodded. "That's right."

"But how did our family get owls as protectors? I mean, did someone in the old days just assign us owls and someone else got, like, pigs?"

"Of course not," Jonah said wearily. "After they died, our ancestors returned as *pueo*, Hawaiian owls, and they take care of us because we're family. Good night, now."

Sure, that explains everything, Darby thought as his footfalls faded away.

Her sleeping bag lay close enough to the pen's fence that she could slip her fingers inside and wiggle them.

She did, but Hoku didn't come to investigate.

Last night as she'd fallen asleep in her new bedroom, Darby had heard hoofbeats. Hoku had trotted endless circles, checking out her new home. Now the filly stood still, head hanging.

So much could change in a day.

Whose fault was it that Hoku had broken out of her paddock? Kimo's, for not repairing the old gate bolt? Her own, for not refastening the bungee cord when she first thought it looked too loose? Jonah's, for putting Hoku in that paddock in the first place?

Jonah hadn't reprimanded anyone—at least not within her hearing. He must have thought it had been a pure accident, or he surely would have assigned blame.

Sighing, Darby looked up the hill toward Sun House. Upstairs and down, the lights were out. The foreman's house, which Kit and Cade shared, had been dark for a long time, though Kit had left the porch light shining.

Had Jonah said anything to Kit about not bringing the stallion Luna up on time? Did Cade's chest
ache where Hoku had bruised him? Was Megan mad
that she hadn't stayed to help with the dishes? And
what about Kit's arm? He'd definitely favored it
when he'd mounted Biscuit.

In their kennel, the dogs paced and scratched,
wondering why she was outside and they weren't.

Hoku still hadn't moved. Her head drooped past
her knees.

She's exhausted, Darby thought.

Night birds called. Dark horse shapes moved all
around the ranch, teeth clipping grass. Small creatures rustled through the brush, coming up or going
down the face of the bluff. Probably searching for
food now that daytime predators were asleep.

Lying on her back, looking into the night sky,
Darby saw a bat. At least, she thought she did. She
blinked, trying to make out the cookie-cutter scallop
of bat wings.

That's not what she saw.

Hoku snorted and Darby sat up, staring into the
sky until her eyes stung.

It was an owl. Silently it passed overhead, sailed
up the road, and merged with the darkness of the
trees that grew by the old fox cages.

Darby rolled over on her side and smiled into the
darkness.

If an owl had come out to protect her, it must

think she was a real Kealoha.

Her eyelids grew heavy, and then she was asleep, but her dream was far from restful.

In Darby's nightmare, she rode Hoku on a Los Angeles freeway, against traffic. Horns blared, then whined into the distance as cars raced past. She wanted to turn right. Or left. Anything but trot toward the onrushing traffic.

"If I can't find the path, you can. Jonah promised you knew the way home!"

Even as she said it, she knew her dream self was wrong. It was Navigator who knew the way home, not Hoku. The filly tried to please the dream Darby, looking everywhere for the sagebrush and white *playas* of Nevada, but she was lost.

Merciless, the dream Darby kicked Hoku, making her gallop toward the monsters. The mustang braved the loud metal beetles scrabbling toward her, enduring their hot breath.

Hoku veered toward the edge of the road, tripped, and then she was falling, rolling down an endless hillside as ghosts popped out of caves and swirled around her. In the dream, Hoku brought her forelegs up to cover her head. Her mouth moved in a silent plea. *Don't hurt me. Please, please, please . . .* and then came a cone of white water and a thunderous splash.

Darby's eyes snapped open.

It was still night. Moonlight shone on fence rails. Beyond them stood her sleeping horse.

I'm sorry, Darby thought. Guilt weighed on her like a heavy backpack. Her dream of Hoku in trouble could be because she'd learned of Shan Stonerow's abuse. But she'd been the one riding the filly down the freeway.

Darby gripped the cell phone she'd taken to bed with her. She could call her mom, but how mean would that be?

Mommy, I had a bad dream. Darby mocked herself. Thousands of miles away, her mom wouldn't be able to do a thing about it. Besides, it was about . . . she flipped open the phone to check the time. It was eleven o'clock here. That meant it was two o'clock in the morning in Pacific Pinnacles, on the day Mom was leaving for the shoot in Tahiti. She couldn't call.

Darby rose up on her elbow and peered into the corral. Hoku stood exactly where she'd seen her last.

"Good night, good girl," Darby whispered.

The next time Darby woke, it was raining.

She pulled the sleeping bag over her head and tried to go back to sleep. Raindrops plopped on the sleeping bag, keeping her awake. Finally, she looked at the cell phone clock. It shone in the dark, telling her it was 4:25 in the morning.

Just as she had before, Darby raised up on her elbow and peered into the corral.

She couldn't see Hoku.

"No big deal." She said the words aloud, trying to make herself believe them.

It wasn't like the injured filly could have gone anywhere.

Wincing as rain pelted her forehead, Darby wiggled out of the sleeping bag and tiptoed barefoot through the mud. She grabbed the nearest fence rail for balance and looked inside.

Where was Hoku?

She'd have a better view of the pen if she climbed up higher.

Her bare foot slipped on the lowest wooden rail, but she kept going until she could see over the top. It was so dark. The front porch light from Kit and Cade's house was the only brightness for miles.

No. That darker patch on the floor of the pen couldn't be Hoku. It wasn't big enough. And it wasn't moving.

Squinting through the darkness, Darby put all her imagination into lying to herself. That shape wasn't Hoku. It looked like an extra large trash bag, spread out with a few lumps in it. Hoku could never be that flat and lifeless. The bag had just blown in there from somewhere. Hoku's pen was empty.

A sudden spate of windblown rain lashed Darby's cheek. As she pushed her long hair from her eyes, she saw a rising paleness flutter on the ground. Its movement stopped as soon as the wind did.

Hoku's tail.

"Get up!" Darby clapped her hands. The shape didn't move.

Darby turned to run up to the house, but a rock stabbed the arch of her bare foot and she yelped.

Hearing the noise, a dog barked.

Don't go inside the corral with that horse under any circumstances.

Jonah's voice rang as if he'd just spoken, but Darby fumbled with the latch in the darkness. She was going in there, anyway.

What would it matter if Jonah sent her home, if Hoku was dead?

 Chapter 15

$\mathcal{H}$oku lay on her side, flaxen tail fanned out, head flat on the earth, mouth open.

Darby knelt on the muddy ground in front of the mustang.

Don't touch her. Don't scare her.

Curving her hands at her temples, cupping them above her eyes, Darby tried to block the rain as she searched for a sign of life. Screaming Hoku's name would startle her into jerking her head up on her injured neck.

But why didn't Hoku know Darby was there, just three feet away?

The desire to yell bubbled up in Darby's throat. She had to know if her horse was alive.

Darby's knees sank deeper in the mud as she leaned forward, reaching out, hoping she'd feel the filly's breath on her fingers.

The mustang's eyes snapped open before Darby's elbow had even straightened. A gasp made the white star move on Hoku's chest, but she didn't stir a hoof or an ear.

"Hoku," Darby whispered. "You have to get up, girl."

Raindrops rebounded from the filly's side and neck. Hoku's forelock floated on the surface of the puddle beneath her head and her eyelids fluttered, trying to watch Darby.

An awful wave of guilt washed over Darby as she thought of the splash in her dream. Had that been Hoku falling down? Had she been lying here for hours? She couldn't be sure. Reality, imagination, and dreams were all braided together.

Hoku sneezed. She must have breathed in puddle water.

Hoku coughed and Darby tried to brace the filly's slender neck. Hoku's throat was warm beneath the wet hair and her pulse pounded clear and strong against Darby's palms, but the horse groaned.

Each cough and sneeze stabbed Hoku's injured neck with agony—Darby could almost feel it.

What can I do? Darby ordered her mind to present solutions.

Go for help. Yes, but the filly was weakened by

capture, her sea journey, unfamiliar food, and the injury to her neck. If weariness overtook her, if she quit sneezing and coughing the water away, Hoku could drown.

Move her? Darby knew she wasn't strong enough. Even if she were, tugging and jerking could harm the horse further.

Hold the mustang's head on her lap? That would keep it out of the water, but the filly would jerk away from Darby's touch, damaging her neck even more.

C'mon, you're supposed to be so smart. Darby railed at herself, and the answer popped into her mind.

She could drain the puddle and then run for help. That was it!

Digging like a dog, Darby jammed her hands into the mud at the edge of the puddle. A rivulet, then a stream of rain water followed her fingers. She clawed a trench leading downhill and then the water was rushing, making a streambed of its own, disappearing under the fence.

It worked, but it was only enough for now. Darby got to her feet.

"I'll be right back, girl. I'm not leaving you."

Darby slipped through the gate and locked it behind her. She ran in the beam of light from Kit and Cade's porch and, panting, pounded on their door.

She hadn't even caught her breath when the door jerked inward. Both cowboys stood pulling on shirts, hair awry, eyes narrowed, but awake, already focused on unknown disaster.

"Hoku's down," Darby said. "I don't think she can get up, and she's breathing in water from the rain puddles."

"She's breathing, then," Kit said. Leaning against the porch wall, he pulled on socks and boots. "Is she tossing her head like she wants to rise?"

"No. All she did was sneeze, and it really hurt her."

Kit stomped his feet down into his boots, pulled on his hat, then said, "Let's go see what we can do."

Darby couldn't guess what instinct had pulled Jonah from bed and into the night, but he was approaching the corral just ahead of them.

In a few short exchanges, he and Kit agreed the best thing to do was cover the filly with blankets and leave her alone.

Why was calling a vet out of the question, when Jonah had paid a farrier just yesterday? Darby asked again and again, but the only answer that made sense was Cade's; examination by another strange human would traumatize the filly even more.

Jonah told Darby how to sponge clean water into Hoku's mouth, and the filly licked the moisture from her lips every time.

He directed her how to bandage Hoku's knees, too.

"Lying in the mud that way, they could get infected," he said.

By eight o'clock, Darby's hands were numb, but not from the cold. She'd been massaging Hoku ever since she'd noticed that the hot, swollen muscle in the filly's neck seemed cooler and less pronounced. Hoku's relaxation was so complete, at first Darby thought she was unconscious, but the mustang welcomed her touch.

Don't waste these first weeks when she's most vulnerable, Jonah had said, and though Darby had resented the way he'd said it, *what* he'd said had turned out to be true.

The filly raised her eyelids.

Yes, Darby thought, *Jonah was right.* How else could she explain a wild filly looking at her this way?

In dawn's silver light, she saw maybe not trust, yet, but acceptance.

"I'll be here when you need me, Hoku," Darby whispered, then sat back on her heels. While she tried to shake the feeling back into her hands, Darby drank in the wonder of her horse.

Hoku stared at her expectantly, uttered a low nicker, and Darby returned to rubbing the mustang's muscles.

By ten o'clock, Darby and Hoku were surrounded by a bright blue and white morning, but Darby's hope was faltering. Hoku still showed no sign of rising.

The puddles had nearly all vanished, when Jonah tossed hay over the corral fence and Hoku's legs pumped back and forth.

"She's hungry," he said. "See if she'll eat."

She did.

Straw by straw, Darby fed the filly. Hoku chewed a dozen mouthfuls before shifting her nose away and closing her eyes.

Hoku slept soundly, and though Kit, Cade, and Jonah went to work, Darby didn't leave her filly's side. Her legs and shorts had been caked with mud. Now, it had dried and the dirt flaked off each time she moved. Darby didn't care.

It wasn't hunger or fear that finally got Hoku up again. It was annoyance.

Pip, the little white dog, had snatched a lead rope from somewhere. Although it was nearly as thick as her own small body, Pip thought it was a great toy. She zipped around the ranch, teasing the Australian shepherds into chasing her.

Hoku's ears flattened as the dogs barked and sped up and down the rolling hills.

"Irritation's a good sign," Darby told the horse, though it was only a guess. At least Hoku's eyes were open and darting around, instead of dull and dazed.

When Pip saw an escape route open only to her, she dove under the bottom rail of Hoku's pen. Unconcerned with the girl and horse, the terrier tugged, growled, and tried to pull the rope inside, too.

Once again, Hoku's legs churned, but this time

her head heaved up from the ground. The filly bared her teeth in pain, but her shoulder muscles strained and her hind legs thrashed.

What should I do? Darby dodged the flailing hooves and positioned herself as Jonah had yesterday, with her hands against the filly's back.

Hoku's spine arched against Darby's palms before the filly rolled panting to her belly. Her front legs cocked up, trembling, bent at her bandaged knees.

When the muscles in Hoku's hindquarters tensed, Darby got out of the way.

The filly lurched and struggled into unhorselike contortions. Finally she was up.

Hoku's ears flattened in anger and Pip, seeing how things were going, scooted back under the fence to escape.

For three days, Darby refused to leave her horse, except to go to the bathroom.

Her days settled into a routine. She woke up, checked on Hoku, and rolled her sleeping bag, wrapping it three times around with its leather string, then stashed it in the tack room.

She groomed Hoku and massaged her neck. She talked on Jonah's cell phone to her mother, who never failed to lecture her about calling Mrs. Allen *right now*, and she sat watching the wild filly, trying to build her trust.

Although Darby had Jonah's cell phone to tell time, the eleven o'clock flight of the owl and the call of the stallion Luna were just as accurate. Each night at 12:40 and 2:30, the stallion's raspy, demanding neigh carried up the bluff from his pasture.

Several times each day, Aunty Cathy or Megan brought Darby meals. Sometimes they delivered little stir-fried concoctions in pretty plastic bowls, but usually they carried sandwiches. Often, Darby tore into them as if she were starving. Other times, she let them sit until the bread curled up at the edges, then sneaked them to the dogs.

She was so obsessed, so totally dedicated to the filly, it was almost like they were both sick.

Kimo stopped by to bring Darby bottles of water. Even though the clouds drizzled rain on her at least twice each day, she was usually thirsty and she welcomed his good-natured company.

"She's givin' me the stink eye," Kimo commented when Hoku glared at him. And he always asked Darby what sounded like, "You pow?"

Darby shrugged off the question until she finally remembered to ask Megan if she knew what he meant.

"*Pau* is Hawaiian for 'are you finished?' or 'all done?,'" Megan explained.

"With Hoku?" Darby had gasped.

"I guess," Megan told her.

Finished with Hoku! Of course she wasn't.

But at least she understood. Megan gave her a teasing smile and added, "You'll pick it up bumbye."

"By and by?" Darby guessed, but Megan was walking away.

She had a lot to write in her notebook, if she ever got back to it, Darby thought.

And the next time Kimo asked, "You *pau* with that horse?" Darby shot back, "No way."

Cade stopped by so often—about once an hour, it seemed—that Darby got used to his vaquero shirts and ponchos. He hadn't said much after she turned down his first offer to help, but he didn't seem offended.

"She's holding her head level with her withers," Cade pointed out on the third morning after Hoku's escape.

They were watching Hoku nip at bright green hay from a net mounted on the wall of her pen.

"She's stiff, but looking a lot more normal," Darby agreed, and then they were joined by Aunty Cathy carrying a paper plate of fried Spam and eggs.

"Wash those hands first," Cathy ordered as Darby reached for her breakfast.

Darby would have laughed at being treated like a two-year-old if her hands hadn't been so grubby.

She'd started over to rinse her hands under the spigot at the horse trough when she heard a strange sound. Probably a bird.

"What's that?" she asked.

Aunty Cathy knew immediately.

"A wild turkey. I saw her earlier this morning, over near those trees. Listen to her." Cathy shook her head at the loud gobbling. "It's no wonder hawks eat her chicks. She started out with six under her skirts and now she's only got two."

Cade pushed back from the fence and walked off without a word.

"What is *up* with him?" Darby asked.

Cathy considered the question a few seconds, then said, "You couldn't blame Cade for being a little jealous. Not that he is, but he could be."

"Of me? Why?" Darby asked.

If Cade hadn't hinted his father beat him, she couldn't have summoned up even a pinch of sympathy for a guy who attended school through the mail, had been "taken in" by the owner of a two thousand-acre ranch, and rode an Appaloosa that danced like a circus horse.

"Jonah was training him to be a paniolo and Cade soaked up lessons like he was born to it. He knows more about paniolo history and skills than anyone this side of the Bishop Museum."

Darby chewed thoughtfully for a minute, then asked, "*Was* training him? Why did he stop?"

"He'll get back to it, but things haven't been the same since we lost Ben, and then Jonah persuaded your mom to let you come. And now Hoku . . ." Cathy wet her lips. "Knowing Jonah, he probably implied

Cade would be in line to take charge of the ranch someday, and that's on the boy's mind, too."

Aunty Cathy had said the same thing about her husband and Pani.

"I don't get it. Jonah isn't that old. Why is he so worried about who'll run the ranch after he's gone?"

"It soothes me," Jonah said.

Darby jumped at her grandfather's interruption and sudden appearance, then asked, "What does?"

"Pretending I can control the future," Jonah told her.

Darby didn't know what was pretend about it. Wasn't that why people went to attorneys and made out wills?

Aunty Cathy gave a wave and strode off toward the house, as if she didn't want to be part of this conversation.

"Well, I better get back to work," Darby said, but she couldn't help noticing that Hoku didn't turn to look toward her voice as she usually did. She stood at the far fence, staring west.

"We all have moods," Darby said when she saw that Jonah, too, had noticed Hoku's indifference.

"You've wanted a horse your whole life, yeah? But maybe she hasn't always wanted a human." Jonah lifted his chin in the direction of Navigator, standing saddled across the ranch yard. "His whiskers are trimmed, his bridle path neatened, and he's ready to go for a ride."

"But Hoku—"

"Catch a hint, Darby." Jonah pretended to plead with her. "Give poor Hoku a rest."

He probably knew best, Darby admitted to herself. And she didn't want Navigator to forget he liked her.

"Okay," she said, "I guess me and Gator will be hitting the trail."

She was smiling, until Jonah gave a long-suffering sigh.

"What?" Darby asked. Couldn't she do anything right?

"I'm just a superstitious old man, but I was raised to think you insult someone when you shorten his name. Even a horse."

Insult him? Darby wondered if this was another superstition like the owls and little people, but she said, "By calling him Gator, I was just being friendly."

"Navigator's got racing Quarter Horse blood just like her majesty over there." Jonah gestured toward Hoku. "And those rusty marks around his eyes and nostrils? *He* comes by them naturally, but some mainland Indian tribes painted those on war ponies so they'd see and smell trouble coming."

"I think he's a great horse!" Darby insisted.

"I know." Jonah's tone changed to approval. "And he thinks you're great, too, or he wouldn't have picked you."

Gee, too bad she hadn't had time to tell her mom that Jonah was trying to drive her crazy. She bet she could have gotten some sympathy.

Jonah walked with Darby to the hitch rail, then led Navigator over to the side hill where he'd watched her mount up before. She made it into the saddle with so little flapping and commotion, Navigator didn't swing his head around to stare.

"Ride wherever you want," Jonah said. "This horse earned his name by reading the sky from any-place on this island."

A breeze smelling of rain blew the ends of Darby's ponytail against her cheek.

"What about my—" She broke off. All at once her shyness returned and she ran all the words together in a rush to get them out. "CathysaidIhaveagreat-grandmother?" Jonah didn't look bewildered, so she added, "Is she near enough that I could—"

"You'll meet *Tutu* when you're ready," Jonah said.

His tone implied that that wouldn't be today, and Darby didn't insist. She'd grown up with no relatives except her mom, and she was already having trouble understanding this one new family member standing before her.

"Okay," Darby said, shifting her gaze to the end of the driveway. She felt the pull of trails that squiggled down the face of the bluff to pastures unrolling like kelly-green carpet.

"But if you happen to find your way to her house," Jonah called after her, "Navigator will bring you home again."

As she rode away, Darby thought it was pretty weird that she'd already heard those words in her dream.

Chapter 16

When she returned from her ride, Darby noticed Kit playing a light spray from the hose over a sturdy palomino.

I shouldn't be envying that horse, Darby thought as she drew rein by the hitching rail.

"Navigator," she said to her horse, "if I don't take a shower pretty soon, we're going to smell exactly alike."

"Who says you don't now?" Kimo said as Darby dismounted.

Darby stuck her tongue out at him.

Kimo jerked a thumb toward his truck.

"I'm going into town to get a part for the ATV, yeah? Want to come?"

188 • Wild Horse Island

"I can't," Darby said. "Hoku—" She broke off with a shrug.

"Want me to pick anything up for you?" Kimo offered.

Darby bit her lip. Her world had shrunk to Hoku and the round pen. She really, truly couldn't think of anything she needed.

"No, but thanks," she said, and then when Kimo offered to untack Navigator for her, Darby decided that before she went back to Hoku, she'd hurry up to the house for a shower.

Darby pulled off her boots as soon as she reached the entrance hall, then listened to the footsteps overhead. Aunty Cathy had gone up to her apartment. That meant Darby had the house to herself.

She blinked her sun-dazzled eyes as she went down the hall to her bedroom. She gathered an armload of fresh clothes, then stopped and considered her bedside clock.

It would be dinnertime in Nevada, and her mom had sworn that if she phoned tonight and Darby still hadn't called to thank Mrs. Allen, she'd take "drastic measures." Darby couldn't guess what those would be from Tahiti, but calling Mrs. Allen was the polite thing to do. After all, Mrs. Allen had taken Hoku in when she was hurt and half-frozen, and she'd been the first to suggest that Darby should adopt the wild filly.

And since Jonah had given her permission to

make the call two days ago, Darby had run out of excuses.

She headed for the kitchen phone and stopped in the doorway.

Jonah stood in front of the open refrigerator drinking from a carton of milk.

"Caught me," he said, wiping his mouth with the back of his wrist. "Might as well finish it off, I guess."

Darby couldn't explain, even to herself, why she watched while he poured the rest of the milk into a glass and stirred in powdered chocolate.

"Want some?" he asked.

She shook her head, then pointed at the phone.

"Go ahead," he told her, and sat down at the round kitchen table with his chocolate milk.

He's doing this to annoy me, she thought. *But it is his kitchen.*

"Th-thanks," she said. She hated the idea of performing this call before an audience, but it wasn't like she had anything secret to say.

"Hello?" Mrs. Allen answered right away. Her voice painted an instant picture for Darby.

She imagined the old lady, with her ink-black hair pulled to the nape of her neck to show big silver earrings. She looked like the eccentric artist she was, but she'd turned a ruined cattle ranch into a wild horse sanctuary, and now she was engaged to a retired policeman. Darby thought she was amazing.

"Mrs. Allen? This is Darby Carter, and I—"

"Well, Darby." Mrs. Allen's greeting was as warm as a hug.

"Thanks so much for sending Judge over with my horse."

"Is Judge enjoying his Hawaiian vacation, then? After all his years of labor, he deserves it, don't you think?"

"Yes, and it was so nice of you."

"And what if I said it was a bribe, so that you'd stay in touch with a lonely old woman?"

Darby hesitated. She knew Mrs. Allen was kidding, but no amusing answer came to mind. "Of course I'll stay in touch."

"With Samantha Forster, too, I hope," Mrs. Allen said. "She took quite an interest in you, since you two are like peas in a pod when it comes to horses. 'Course, you remind me of Jen Kenworthy a bit, too. You're both just too darn smart for most normal purposes."

Racing to catch each of Mrs. Allen's words was hard enough, but making sense of them was nearly impossible.

"Sam sent me a fax," Darby blurted.

"About that filly of yours?"

"Yes—"

"Well, I heard all about her ancestry, and even pretty as she is, I hope you're being careful."

"I'm careful," Darby insisted, turning away from the table as Jonah looked up with raised eyebrows.

"Well, there's bad blood in that line of horses. Bad blood no one talks about, because it sounds like superstition. It's not. My first husband caught your filly's—" Mrs. Allen's voice broke off in a whisper. Darby wondered if she was talking to someone else, then realized the old lady was counting generations of horses. "There was Smoke, and his sire was that tall running gray, but *his* sire was a white renegade with murder in his eyes. He'd be your filly's great-great-grandsire. Not that it matters, except—I know she's sweet as pie with you, but has she hurt anyone?"

Darby hesitated. Then, since Jonah already knew, she admitted, "There was a little bit of trouble, right when she first got here, but Sam told me she was abused by a man—"

"That may well be, but she could be a throw-back—"

"A throwback?" Darby echoed. She'd never heard the expression.

"—to that outlaw stallion that attacked my husband. Once every three or four generations, one of them's born just hateful."

"My horse isn't—"

"Don't be too sure, is all I'm saying. That stud had us fooled. I saw with my own eyes how he was snubbed to a post—this was before BLM said you couldn't catch horses off the range—and he looked perfectly gentle and soft-eyed. Then all at once he rose up like a grizzly bear, pulled the post out of the

ground, and set off after the men. Caught my husband and gave him a big purple heart-shaped bruise.

"That stud struck out at him with a front hoof just
like a bear with its claws, too. I'll tell you, honey, it
was the strangest thing. That bruise faded, but never
truly went away."

Darby gasped, thinking of Cade's bruise. But
heart-shaped? That couldn't be true.

Mrs. Allen broke off her dramatic narrative with
a chuckle and added, "I won't tell you precisely *where*
he wore that mark for the rest of his days. Suffice it
to say, he was running away from the horse when he
got it!"

The old lady sighed at her memories and Darby
cast a quick glance at Jonah, happy he couldn't hear
Mrs. Allen's side of the conversation.

"Well, my horse is settling down," Darby insisted.

"All right, dear. You stay in touch, now. You
sound more chipper than before and I'm happy for it.
Us crazy horse ladies need to stick together, don't
we?"

"Yeah," Darby said. She heard the low rumble of
a male voice near Mrs. Allen.

"My fiancé"—Mrs. Allen drew out the word in a
showy manner—"says hello and wants me to remind
you that we told your lovely mother that you could
call us if you need anything at all."

"Thank you," Darby said automatically.

"You will, won't you?" Mrs. Allen asked. "Why,

now that I'm about to marry money, the sky's the limit!" Mrs. Allen didn't say good-bye, but Darby heard the telephone receiver jumble down into place, and she hung up, too.

Taking a deep breath, Darby turned to face Jonah, wondering how much he'd puzzled together from what she'd said.

"Throwback, huh?"

Of course Jonah would hear that part!

He walked over to the sink and ran water into his empty glass before Darby could read his expression.

"Sometimes in wild herds, like the one in Crimson Vale, you get that, too." He shook his head. "Traits that should die out get magnified instead."

"It's just an old superstition." Darby struggled to use an exaggeratedly creepy voice as she said, "Bad blood emerges from the shadows every three or four generations." She cleared her throat, then added, "Totally made up."

Darby knew her acting skills weren't great, but she thought she'd managed to sound unimpressed with Mrs. Allen's story.

"Most superstitions are." Jonah paused and Darby's shoulders sagged in relief until he added, "*Old*, that is. But that doesn't mean they're not true."

Darby headed for the shower and tried to block out Jonah's remark by listing things she should have asked Kimo to buy for her.

How could she have forgotten that she shared a bathroom with Jonah?

It's not that I'm a girly girl, Darby thought, but her mom had always kept their cabinets stocked with the basics. Lotion, shampoo, and conditioner, nothing fancy, just whatever was on sale, but now Darby appreciated them, because Jonah apparently used bars of harsh brown soap for everything.

She was ready to climb into the shower, when there was a knock at the bathroom door.

Darby grabbed a towel, then opened the door to Aunty Cathy.

"Thought you might like these." She handed Darby bottles of shampoo and conditioner.

"You're psychic!" Darby said happily.

"And this," Aunty Cathy said, offering a glass.

While Darby tried to find a place for everything without dropping her towel, Cathy said, "It's a mango milkshake."

"Oh my gosh."

"Welcome back to civilization."

"I'm only visiting," Darby said, "but thanks so much!"

After her shower, Darby dressed in fresh clothes. All the time she was zipping and buttoning, her eyes caressed her bed. One corner of the blanket was folded down to show crisp and welcoming white sheets. She really should persuade her heavy, traitorous limbs that there was no real difference between that bed and the rumpled sleeping bag she'd used for the last three nights. But maybe she'd lie down for just a minute.

When Darby awakened, dinner was on the table, so she couldn't exactly turn down eating with "the family" to run back to Hoku. Then she'd heard herself volunteering to help clean the kitchen.

Her mom would be proud, Darby thought, but now Megan was shooting her a sidelong glance as she said, "You should have taken care of your own horse." Megan ran water over a dish, then added, "They were talking about it."

Darby knew who "they" were. From the kitchen window, she could see Kit and Jonah working even though the sun had gone down.

"But I don't know how, really. I've been working with Hoku, and besides, Kimo took Navigator and said he'd take care of him as soon as I rode in."

Darby didn't realize she was chewing on her bottom lip until Megan said, "Your lipstick won't go on smooth if you keep doing that."

Darby laughed, though she could tell Megan was trying to be helpful. She wasn't done talking about Navigator, either.

"Look, it's no big deal. I certainly don't care, but there's this whole paniolo thing where you're judged by the way you treat your horse. Like, my dad used to joke that we were lucky we lived now, because in the old days, paniolo fed their horses before their wives and children, and I thought you'd want to know. Why are you staring at me like that?"

"I'm not. I mean, I'm sorry. Sometimes I do that when I'm trying to think."

"Well, it's creepy." Megan started giggling. "Don't leech my brainpower, cuz. I don't have much to spare."

Then Darby was laughing again. She still didn't know that much about Megan—just that she was pretty and popular, and had been a good rider before she'd given it up. Darby guessed that though Megan tried to be aloof, her friendliness wouldn't allow it.

"So what do you think Jonah would do if I asked him to show me how to do all the stuff I need to learn to take care of my horse?"

"I think he would eat it up. Absolutely," Megan said.

"Now?" Darby asked. She really wanted to get back to Hoku, so she hoped Megan would tell her there was no hurry.

"Sure," Megan said. "It's not like *you* have to go to school in the morning." She snatched the dish towel from Darby and snapped it at her.

"Oh yeah," Darby said, dodging, "but I hear some people do."

She darted out of the kitchen and yanked open the front door.

Hopping from one foot to the other, Darby pulled on her boots. A light drizzle was falling again, and she'd really rather crawl into bed and read, but what if she lost her nerve?

Chapter 17

"Here's what I think we'll do with your filly," Jonah said as Darby held her breath and balanced Navigator's hoof on her knee.

It was late.

So far Jonah had helped her to saddle and bridle a horse, then unsaddle and unbridle him. He'd talked her through grooming Navigator with several brushes and combs and shown her how to gently wipe around his eyes.

Cleaning hooves was supposed to be the last thing Darby learned, but her head was so crammed with unfamiliar words and actions, she had little hope she'd remember anything tomorrow.

Crouching with shaking thigh muscles, she held

the wicked-looking hoof pick poised above Navigator's hoof. Looking up at Jonah for instructions, Darby swallowed a yawn.

Jonah said, "See that vee on the bottom of his foot? That's the frog. It's your horse's nonslip shock absorber. It'll help keep you both safe, so take good care of it," Jonah explained.

"Okay," Darby said.

"Use the tip of the pick to gently remove any mud or dirt that's gotten caked in there. Away," he said sharply, "always pick it away from the heel, toward the toe. Don't take a chance of pushing grit into the sensitive part of the foot.

"I read that fax from the girl in Nevada. She said this Stonerow character tried to train your filly quick and dirty, so I think we should start over and do it clean and slow. Good. Now set that down—easy, don't drop it—and move to the next hoof."

Still facing Navigator's tail, Darby ran her hand down his leg.

"Good boy," she murmured when he lifted the hoof.

"It'll take a year before you're riding her. You need to win her friendship. Teach her general rules of respect. Control her energy."

"Okay," Darby said.

Jonah watched her inspect each of Navigator's hooves. They weren't the least bit dirty because Cade had already cleaned them.

At last Jonah told Darby to release the tall geld-ing to wander with the other saddle horses. Then they walked toward Hoku's corral.

"That kind of work I'm talking about," Jonah said, "it requires isolation. There's a little corral out in the forest. How would you feel—if she stays settled down for you—about working out there with her?"

Isolation wasn't Darby's favorite word. Working alone in a forest sounded even worse.

"Out by Pearl Pasture?" Darby asked, stalling.

"Yeah."

"Going out to the jungle," Darby said. "Is that the only right way to do it?"

"No, there are plenty of right ways, but that's the one that will work best," Jonah said.

Why did he act like she was wasting his time? Darby wondered.

Wide awake, the filly watched them come. The lights picked up her gleaming eyes. But Hoku wasn't alone.

Hatless, Kit stood watching her through the rails. He beckoned them to look, too.

"You see that?" Kit asked.

As soon as she'd recognized Darby and Jonah, Hoku turned away from them all. She pressed her chest against the far fence.

"She does that sometimes," Darby told him. "It helps her calm down."

"Yeah, well, it kinda gets to me," Kit said.

"Why's that?" Jonah asked, and Darby heard the respect in her grandfather's voice.

He didn't think Kit's comments were a waste of time.

"See what she's done? Found West. She's pointin' at it like a compass," Kit said. He smooched at Hoku, but her ears barely flicked at the sound. "Poor critter has no clue she's already so far west she'd have to run around the world to find her home."

Dark loneliness settled over Darby as she lay in her sleeping bag, looking at the stars.

She'd accomplished a lot since she'd been on 'Iolani Ranch. She could ride. She'd cared for an injured horse. She'd learned the names of all the dogs and most of the horses. She'd made friends—sort of—with everyone on the ranch. Why did Jonah always ask for more?

Now that she'd settled into a strange place and felt almost at home, he wanted to exile her to the jungle.

Darby's leg muscles twitched. She pulled her knees up to her chest, then stretched until her toes hit the end of her sleeping bag. Nothing helped her feel less fidgety, and her muscles were nothing compared to her agitated mind.

How could she show Jonah that she and Hoku were making progress right here?

The crunch of a hoof on dirt told her she wasn't

the only one awake. Suddenly she knew what she could do.

"Hoku?" Darby whispered.

The horse breathed louder and more quickly, as if she shared Darby's dangerous thoughts.

"Hoku, can I come in there?"

I shouldn't. I really *shouldn't,* Darby thought, but she worked her way out of the sleeping bag as quietly as she could and took the long leather tie string with her.

Cold nipped at her knees and elbows. As usual, she'd worn loose shorts and a T-shirt for bed. She bit back a gasp as her feet touched the wet grass, but one step later she was climbing the fence.

She didn't want anyone to hear the gate open.

And she couldn't take a chance that Hoku would rush past her and escape again. Her neck couldn't take it, and, though the filly had survived on the high desert range, in wild Hawaii, she wouldn't know what to do.

At the top of the fence, Darby pushed her hair behind her shoulders, swung a leg over, gripped with her toes, and climbed down on the other side.

Hoku knew Darby was up to something.

In the darkness, the mustang's flaxen mane floated away from her neck as she trotted in circles. The circles tightened until it seemed there was a six-foot force field around Darby.

Darby stood stubbornly in the middle of the paddock, even when Hoku bore down on her. The white star on her chest tipped from side to side in time with her strides, but Darby closed her eyes, held her ground. And her breath.

A clacking sound made Darby open one eye.

Hoku had stopped right in front of her and she clacked her teeth. Darby had never seen a horse do that, or even read about it. She had no idea what it meant.

Darby counted to one hundred, then raised her arm slowly from her side.

So far, so good, she thought and opened her hand.

Hoku threw her head up as if Darby had tossed dust in her face. Hoku's neck was still stiff, and she snorted, but she didn't retreat a single step.

"I won't touch your face," Darby promised.

The horse breathed in her scent over and over again, just as she had lying next to her in the December snow. Darby slowly threaded the leather string through a metal loop on Hoku's halter.

Jonah had said it would be weeks before the filly could be led, since they couldn't put an ounce of strain on her neck. But if she could accomplish that now—or in a few moonlight sessions—he'd see that Darby's way worked.

She held the leather string between her thumb and index finger, let it hang loose between her and the filly, then took a step back.

Here you come, Darby exulted in amazement as

Hoku took two steps toward her.

"Good girl!" Darby cheered quietly. "Now, one more."

Darby held out her hand, palm up.

Hoku's head swung from side to side with alert ears. She might have been inspecting figures standing alongside Darby's body. Except that no one was there.

"I don't know what you think you see, but we're alone."

Darby looked over her shoulder, just to be sure, but it was too early for the owl. Darby shivered. There was nothing there.

It was just her luck that Hoku's imagination was as fanciful as hers.

"And that's one more reason I don't want to move your training to the forest," she told Hoku. She kept her hand extended, palm up. "We'll have each other flinching at shadows."

The filly didn't take a third step, but she rocked forward without moving her hooves. Hoku's chin hovered just above Darby's open hand and she stared into the girl's eyes.

"That's my good horse," Darby said, but when Hoku nodded her head to say, *That's my hay-carrying human,* a single whisker grazed Darby's palm. The filly bolted back as if she'd felt an electrical shock.

Darby released the leather string and allowed herself a sigh, but it was no more than a minute before Hoku had circled around behind Darby.

A rumbling nicker came from the filly. Darby smiled, but didn't turn to face her. Warmth radiated from Hoku's body as she came closer. And closer.

Maybe a mustang felt safer with no eyes fixed on her. Maybe that's why Hoku bumped Darby's ear, then nudged her arm.

Reaching behind her, Darby snagged the leather string and took a step away from Hoku. The filly followed, exploring her girl with sniffs and nudging, communicating as horses do. Finally, after they'd walked a full circuit of the corral together, Darby stopped.

Eyes closed, breath as even and slow as she could keep it, Darby stood still as Hoku leaned against her.

Darby and the wild filly stood cheek to cheek, mane to mane.

Worth the wait, Darby thought.

She wished they could stand this way forever.

Chapter 18

After two nights of midnight schooling, uninter-
rupted by people or even the barking of the dogs,
Darby knew Hoku was no renegade or throwback.

The owl knew, too. Almost every time Darby
looked up at the tree shading the old cages, she saw
its foot-high form watching, intent as a round-faced
child. Sometimes the owl dropped from its branch, a
silent swoosh of brown and white feathers, and she
knew it was hunting, because once she heard the surprised squeak of its prey.

After four nights, Darby believed Hoku was the
sweetest filly on earth, a fairy-tale horse who'd fallen
under her enchantment. It happened in books all the
time, but who would have guessed that a wild horse

would do exactly what Darby Carter of Pacific Pinnacles, California, wanted her to?

Working together was making them both stronger. Each minute Darby spent with the filly made her confident that Jonah would eventually come around to her way of thinking.

She imagined leading Hoku out of her pen and right past him on the end of a leather string (a thread would be better, but she'd be humble). The filly would show off a little, prancing and tossing her Rapunzel-like mane as she followed each of Darby's requests.

Jonah would beg for Darby's forgiveness—once he'd recovered from speechless shock—and admit that Hoku had made such progress, there was no reason to banish Darby and her filly to a jungle.

Hoku didn't confide her own dreams, but Darby knew the filly's shining strength could be credited to more than their friendship. From the first bite when she lay sick in the mud, Hoku had developed a passion for hay.

Hoku loved the smell of it, the crunch of it, even the prickle of its stalks against her soft lips. She'd follow Darby anywhere to get the fragrant green food and each night, after Hoku had devoured the hay Darby sneaked to her for training treats, the filly licked Darby's empty palm, savoring what *had* been there. Hoku's tongue tickled Darby's hand until she had to fight off giggles.

Nights with Hoku were magical, but during the day, Darby bit her tongue and listened to Jonah's warnings.

Just that morning, she'd run up to Sun House to change into fresh clothes. She'd been washing her face, staring at a reflection that showed darkly tanned skin and blue eyes so bloodshot she wondered why they didn't hurt, when suddenly she heard Hoku scream.

Heart pounding, Darby had bolted out the front door and downhill past the tack shed.

Was it a neigh of anger or fear? As she sped down the track without her usual glance for the jumble of old cages, she didn't know. Her steps had slowed as she spotted Jonah outside Hoku's pen.

Breathless, Darby said, "She's . . . still afraid of . . . men."

Why had she sounded apologetic? Cade had said it would take time for Hoku to forget what Shan Stonerow had done to her. Darby didn't tell Jonah that, because the glimpse she caught of the filly didn't show a horse that was afraid, but one locked in a battle of wills.

Jonah gave no sign he'd heard her excuse, anyway. With crossed arms, he watched Hoku's ears flash in all directions. She was curious but confused. Why didn't Darby make this man go away?

I will, she thought to the horse.

She's fine at night, when it's just the two of us, Darby

wanted to tell her grandfather. But his black brows were lowered in such a forbidding expression, she just couldn't utter all the brave chatter in her mind.

Wham, wham! Hoku's rear hooves slammed the rails. Didn't the vibration telegraph up her spine to hurt her neck? Darby thought it must, but the filly did it over and over again. Was she standing up for herself since Darby was too much of a wimp to make Jonah leave? Or did the pounding ease her outrage that Jonah wouldn't flee from her mustang threats?

Eyes fixed on the filly, Jonah gave a humorless chuckle and asked, "How'd you manage to make her worse?"

Darby's mouth opened in an O.

Worse? After all the hours of heart-wringing worry? After the days and nights of watching, assessing, planning, and work? Because, yeah, even if she loved it, getting to know Hoku was work! How could he say it was all a waste?

For the first time, Jonah turned away from the corral, smile fading as he took in Darby, frozen by what he'd said.

"It was a joke, Granddaughter."

"I don't care," she said.

Jonah grasped her shoulder and gave it a shake, but Darby resisted, staying stiff.

Did he look surprised because she'd suddenly developed a backbone? Could he see she wasn't a coward?

But there was no hint of admiration in his voice when Jonah said, "Horses' minds aren't simple. She may be afraid of men, but that's not what this kicking's about. If she hasn't tried to hurt you yet—"

Darby shook her head.

"—she will. She can't maintain this level of frustration and not strike out at you. She's accepted you as her leader, but she's running out of patience because you're not taking her away from all this." Jonah's gesture took in the ranch and every living thing on it.

Darby felt a flash of guilt. What if Jonah was right?

Not satisfied with her hesitation, Jonah added, "This is not some story in a book, some horse in a movie that's over in ninety minutes. Don't let yourself believe it is."

Chilled, Darby could only nod, pretending to agree.

Shaking his head, Jonah had walked off. Darby noticed the blunt spurs on his boots and told herself that Jonah didn't know everything there was to know about horses. He was wrong about Hoku. She and the filly were growing closer all the time. Someday she'd ride the wild filly into the wind and, seeing them, Jonah would have to admit that Darby and Hoku weren't just horse and rider—they were friends.

* * *

"Final exam time," Darby said, on the night before she planned to show Jonah what Hoku could do.

Darby smothered a yawn. During the day, Hoku dozed, catching up on sleep she missed, but Darby raked the ranch yard or polished tack, two low-skill jobs Jonah had assigned her until she was willing to ride out and spend more time away from her horse.

Darby placed her hand on the pen gate. She'd secretly oiled its hinges.

Darby looked into the starry sky. If only she could connect the silver dots to form a sign that she was doing the right thing.

The only omen she saw wasn't a good one.

Empty black tree branches spread against the moon.

The owl *always* returned to its perch. It *always* watched Hoku's performance, shifting excitedly back and forth. Darby had counted it as company, imagining its round eyes glittered with approval beneath its feathered widow's peak.

The only time she'd turned her back on the *pueo*, as Jonah called it, was when the owl raised a lethal talon to feed itself a bite of mouse.

Some guardian, Darby thought, *not showing up on the night I might really need a protector.*

Taking a deep breath, Darby swung the gate open, then eased it closed behind her.

Hoku was watching. As usual, the filly waited while Darby approached and threaded the leather string through her halter ring. Then she followed the wondrous scent of hay as Darby led.

When they reached the gate, Hoku stopped.

Don't do it. Darby heard the words so clearly, she thought Kit or Cade had spoken from their porch, but no one was there and other words rang more loudly in Darby's mind: *How'd you manage to make her worse?*

Carefully, she considered Hoku. The filly looked relaxed, no more excited than usual. She reached out for the hay, but Darby snatched it away. She'd already made up her mind to keep plenty in reserve, in case the filly kicked up a fuss once they were out of the corral. With the filly's injury and the weak leather string to consider, Darby had to depend on bribery, rather than force.

As they slipped from the pen, two of the Australian shepherds barked.

Darby winced and her shoulders hunched up almost to her ears as they hadn't done in days.

"Quiet," she whispered.

There was another bark, less menacing since they knew it was her. Then she heard the sound of a dog turning around in the kennel, before settling with a grunt.

Darby switched her attention back to Hoku. Usually, the filly followed slowly at the end of the leather string, but she'd caught up. She walked alongside Darby and she wasn't reaching for the hay.

The filly took a deep breath. Smelling horses,

Darby thought, and she waved the hay beneath Hoku's nose. With an irritated snort, Hoku swung her head away, and took two long strides. Darby hurried to keep up.

Okay, that was enough. They were only about ten feet from the pen, but it was time to go back.

Darby smooched to Hoku. The filly's ears didn't flicker. They pointed right ahead as her hooves clipped past the tree.

"We're turning around," Darby whispered. With her thumb and forefinger, she moved the leather string and brushed the hay against Hoku's lips.

Hoku lifted her head higher than she had since the accident, making Darby rise up on her tiptoes to keep hold of the leather.

"You've seen those before." Darby tried to keep her tone calm as the filly checked out the jumble of old cages, but she knew she was losing control.

Hoku swung her head toward the bluff. Her body tensed.

The stallion trumpeted a raspy, demanding neigh from his pasture.

No! It wasn't 12:40 or 2:30! Why had the stallion picked tonight to deviate from his schedule?

But Darby knew why. Luna had sensed Hoku. He was calling to her.

Hoku arched her neck, kicked up her heels, and the leather string slipped through Darby's fingers.

"Hoku, no!" Darby whispered.

The filly stopped and studied her with trembling intensity.

Did the filly know she was loose? Maybe not. Darby blew out the breath she was holding and forced her legs to take casual steps after the horse.

"Here's some hay. Take all of it, pretty girl."

From the apartment above Sun House, Pip began barking. Hoku's ears flattened and she broke into a trot.

Darby dashed after her and once more, the filly arched her neck and bucked with high spirits. She was playing, running because Darby ran, and each time the girl reached for the leather string, the filly sidled away. But when Darby's hand grazed her shoulder, Hoku leaped aside, then disappeared along the trail leading down the bluff.

Okay, if she goes down there, she'll stay with the other horses. That's not so bad, Darby thought, running and puffing.

Then she turned a corner to find Hoku waiting for her.

"Here I am," Darby said, holding out the hay.

The filly came closer and stopped about six feet out of reach, facing Darby, but looking over her head.

Hoku stomped a hoof and lashed her golden tail from side to side, making up her mind.

"Don't go," Darby whispered.

The filly nickered and Darby understood the sound as if the filly had spoken.

You're asking too much, she seemed to say. Then she bolted past Darby at a lope.

"Hoku!" Darby yelled, but the mustang moved faster.

She galloped two widening circles with golden tail lifted, flared, and fluttering behind her as she reached and pulled with corral-cramped muscles. She breathed the salty night wind and tasted freedom.

As Darby ran after her, the filly swiveled her heels toward the stars, and then she ran west.

Chapter 19

Jonah didn't ask how Hoku had escaped. He didn't care *how*, because he knew *who* had allowed it.

It took twenty minutes for Darby to walk back to the ranch from where she'd quit chasing Hoku, and by the time she reached Sun House, three horses were saddled under the tack-room light.

Her breath clawed through lungs that felt abraded, sandpapered from the inside, but when she reached Kit, Cade, and Jonah, each hanging canteens on their saddles, she managed to say, "Let me get Navigator."

"You're staying here," Jonah said. He slapped Kona's belly to make the gray exhale, then yanked the cinch snug and fastened it.

"We'll be riding fast," Cade explained as he mounted Joker.

Astride Biscuit, Kit pulled his black hat lower on his brow, but Darby didn't miss his disappointed frown.

"If you could have seen her," Darby blurted. "She knows she's mine. She wanted me to go with her. . . ."

It had never been so clear that she was living among strangers. No one said a word. Darby apologized so many times Jonah told her to stop.

"This is the last time she'll get out, ever," Darby promised.

"I'll see to that," Jonah said. "That horse was your responsibility, but now she's mine."

"What do you mean?" Darby gasped.

"Everyone on the island knows Jonah Kaniela Kealoha took in a *pupule* mustang from Nevada. I can't have her running through town dodging cars and causing accidents or trampling some farmer's taro patch, eating all he's got in the world. Once she's caught, she'll stay caught."

Then, they rode away.

All day, Darby stayed in her room. She read, made entries in her notebook, straightened all her clothes in her drawers, and read some more. She didn't allow herself to cry. When Jonah got back, she didn't want him to see her with swollen eyes. Plus, she was afraid that once she started crying, she wouldn't be able to stop.

Darby wished she could sleep, even pulled the sheets up over her face. But the sun sifting through her window, making leaf shadows do a crazy dance that she could see through her eyelids, kept her awake.

Even when afternoon clouds moved in, she couldn't nap, because she was listening for Hoku's hooves. If Jonah brought the filly back safely, she'd never break any of his rules ever again.

At three thirty, no horses or riders had returned, but Darby heard the doors slam on the ranch truck as Aunty Cathy brought Megan home. A few minutes later, there was a rap, and Aunty Cathy shouted, "Quit moping. Come upstairs and have some tea with us."

Before Darby could refuse, Cathy was gone.

Moping, she thought while she brushed her hair. Didn't that imply pouting? She wasn't doing either of those. She was depressed because, despite her much-complimented intelligence, she'd done something so stupid, if she lived a hundred years, she probably wouldn't top it.

At least, she really hoped not.

Darby could already hear the tinkle of wind chimes as she trudged up the staircase to Megan and Cathy's apartment.

The door stood open. As she walked in, Darby thought again how much the apartment felt like a tree house, perched up so high, with its fern-patterned screens and wicker furniture.

"Have a seat," Cathy said, and Darby settled into the rocking chair positioned against the wall with the collection of ukuleles, hula dancer dolls, and flowerpots.

Megan lay sprawled on a window seat that Darby hadn't noticed before. She was reading a skinny book, but as Darby sat, Megan flipped it to her.

"I brought you this," Megan said.

Amazing herself, Darby caught the book, and discovered it was a course catalog listing all the classes at Lehua High School.

"Thanks," Darby said, and grateful to have a place to hide from impossible questions, she concentrated on the catalog, even after Cathy handed her a glass of iced tea.

"We should do something tomorrow," Megan offered. "Since it's Saturday."

"Okay," Darby said, but she knew that she'd spend the day with Hoku, if Jonah let her.

"If they don't get back tonight, you're going to have to help with the animals," Cathy told Megan.

"Who's out there now? Just Kimo?" Megan asked.

"Yes," Cathy said.

"Good thing he's the worker bee."

Megan's joking tone made Darby look up. "Worker bee?"

"After Pani left and we lost Ben," Cathy said, "it

crossed Jonah's mind that Kimo might take over running the place, but it didn't take long before he told Jonah that he's just a worker bee. He doesn't want to be the boss."

Why was Jonah so concerned about who'd take over the ranch after he was gone?

When she'd asked the question before, Cathy hadn't given her much of an answer. Looking at Cathy now, Darby's heart began to beat hard. She couldn't have explained why, but later she thought it must have been warming up for what came next.

"So that only leaves Ellen," Cathy said.

Darby only knew one Ellen. Her mother. But that didn't make sense.

"Ellen, my mom?" she asked. What could her mom have to do with running the ranch?

Megan sat up on the window seat and hugged her knees to her chest. With her chin on the shelf of her knees, she watched Darby as Cathy nodded.

"Only leaves her for what?" Darby asked.

"This." Cathy made a circling gesture that took in the whole ranch. "'Iolani Ranch."

Darby sat back so fast, the rocking chair struck the wall behind her. One of the ukuleles swung loose from its hook, hitting a hula doll, which began to jiggle.

"I d-don't think she knows," Darby managed.

"Oh, she knows," Cathy said. "Jonah built this apartment for her, for both of you, when your parents split up. He wrote to Ellen about it, thinking if she didn't have to live in the same house with him, she might come home."

Once before Darby had felt dizzy and disconnected like this. She'd been laughing in a fun house with her mother and they'd stood side by side, staring into a wavy mirror. Darby guessed she must have been pretty little, because her own reflection hadn't scared her like her mother's. Mom had looked unrecognizable, weird.

"Ben and Megan and I lived in the foreman's house—and then just Megan and I did. But when Kit was hired on as foreman, and after your mom still didn't come for almost twelve years, Jonah decided—"

"My mother was never coming back here," Darby finished for her. "I don't think she will, either. She says she hates it. She calls it 'that godforsaken place.'"

Now that she'd seen 'Iolani Ranch with her own eyes, Darby thought her mom was insane to leave forever, no matter what kind of feud she had with her father.

Cathy pointed to the desk in the corner and Darby remembered looking at it when she'd been in the apartment before. She'd thought the only thing that looked out of place was a desk shoved into a corner with two round hatboxes stacked on top.

"Those are hers, the desk and the things in the hatboxes," Cathy said. "There's not much, but since this was supposed to be your mother's little house, you can move in here, and Megan and I can take your room."

Darby sat back fast again, but this time she only slopped tea out of her glass.

"No," Darby said. "I mean, it's great, but . . ." She shook her head and looked down at the wet spot spreading on her jeans. "No way would I evict you. My room's fine."

The late-afternoon rains had begun, and Darby's mind wandered. She wondered how different her life would have been if she'd grown up in this sunny little house on a horse ranch in Hawaii.

Her eyes returned to the small wooden desk.

"Aunty Cathy," she said, because using a family name felt right, "I would like to look through the stuff in the boxes."

"I thought you might," Cathy said.

Before Darby moved, though, she heard barking. She ran to the apartment door and looked outside through the drizzle.

Jonah was back, without Hoku.

Dusk had fallen and Jonah was at the tack shed, stripping the saddle off Kona. Darby hadn't known how much she'd just assumed Jonah would find her horse, until now.

The big gray blew through his lips as Jonah peeled the bridle from his head, gave him a carrot, and turned him out.

Maybe Cade and Kit were riding on each side of the filly, bringing her home slowly.

When Jonah turned toward Darby, she remembered one of the first things she'd thought about her grandfather was that he looked like a man with a concealed weapon.

He still did, and tonight that weapon was his fury. Jonah's frown went beyond his face, down to the cords standing out in his tanned neck. Instead of wearing off during the day, his anger at her had grown.

"How's it, boss?" Kimo said, emerging from the office.

Hands on his hips, Jonah shook his head. "We split up at noon. Cade went downshore. Kit headed toward the valley. I scoured our pastures. No sign of her."

Darby tried to believe Cade and Kit would have better luck. They were younger than Jonah and probably had better eyes.

"Here comes Kit on a lame horse," Jonah snapped suddenly.

Darby squinted in the direction in which Jonah was looking. Without meaning to, she released a shaky sigh. Another horse hurt because of her.

Kit dismounted while he was still on the road next to the house, then walked slowly toward them.

"Biscuit spooked and slid in the mud before we

even got into the valley," Kit said as he approached, leading the horse.

"What at?" Jonah asked.

"Didn't see a thing. Could have been one of those wild horses, a bird, or maybe he was just tired and lost track of where he was puttin' his feet." Kit shrugged. "Beats me, but Biscuit's going to need some doctoring. Sorry, boss."

Swallowing hard, Darby said, "You shouldn't apologize. It's my fault you were out there."

No one contradicted her. Kimo and Jonah watched Kit dab yellow ointment on Biscuit's legs, shutting her out, and finally, Darby went back to the ranch office and sat with the door open, because it gave her the best view of the road coming into the ranch.

Almost certainly, this was the way Cade would ride in—with or without Hoku.

No one brought her dinner, and that was okay, because Cathy kept jelly beans in a jar on her desk and Darby had eaten enough of them that she'd have to apologize for that, too.

She was awake for Luna's midnight neigh, and for Jonah driving slowly down the driveway at two A.M.

When he bumped back down the road at 3:14, he drove right up to the office and climbed out of the truck.

"Cade's coming back. Without your horse."

Her heart felt like a rock inside her chest, but she still didn't cry.

"Do you think she can find her way back?" she asked Jonah.

"Hard to tell," he said, and she was pretty sure her grandfather really didn't know.

Nose hanging past his knees and hooves dragging, Joker returned to the ranch looking like a very old horse.

Alarm flashed though Darby. She hadn't thought of how hours of running and searching would affect the little Appaloosa.

Cade slid off his horse, dropped the reins, and walked toward Darby and Jonah as if his feet were swollen in his boots.

The office light cast a pale yellow wash over his face and it almost looked like tears had streaked Cade's dirty face before he'd smeared them with the back of his hand. Had he been *that* sure his paniolo skills would lead him to Hoku?

He looked at the ground as he spoke.

"I found her, then lost her. She was running over rock and it was dark. But I'm pretty sure she didn't fall. . . ." Cade gave such a heavy sigh, Darby thought he'd finished talking.

"When?" Jonah asked.

"Hours ago. It was still light," Cade said. "That's why I kept looking. It didn't seem like she should've dropped out of sight. If she'd fallen, Joker would have heard her." Cade finally looked up. "Or I would've found her. In the morning—"

"Kimo and I will take over in the morning," Jonah said, and when Cade made a sound of protest, he added, "Cade, you need some rest, and so does Joker."

"I'll take another horse," Cade insisted.

"You're no good to me like this, boy. Get to bed and I'll see to your horse. You've nearly run him to death."

Cade recoiled at Jonah's accusation, but it silenced him.

Darby watched Jonah strip the tack from the Appaloosa, right where he stood, in front of the office. Then Cade walked beside Jonah as far as the foreman's house, and let himself be forced inside.

Joker drifted behind them for a few steps, then dropped and rolled, groaning, in the dewy grass.

Carrying the Western saddle and bridle as if they were weightless, Jonah shouldered through the tack-room door.

"I'm sorry," she said when Jonah returned for her.

"I'm sure you are."

He nodded toward Sun House, and since she could see he wouldn't take no for an answer, Darby walked beside him.

An upstairs window went dark as they approached. Either Aunty Cathy or Megan had been waiting up.

Jonah opened the front door and a breeze rushed

from the lanai and swirled around Sun House. He didn't turn on a single light as he walked Darby to her bedroom door, then continued down the hall to his own.

She'd been awake for more than twenty-four hours and she should have fallen asleep right away, but it was a long time before Darby's eyes closed. Even then, she kept wondering what she would tell her mother if Hoku was gone for good.

Chapter 20

Saturday dawned with rainbows and a neigh outside Darby's bedroom window.

Her first thought was of Hoku. During the few hours she'd been in bed, she'd hung between sleep and morbid fantasies. Old dreams of the rain forest and Hoku falling from a cliff kept coming back. Darby forced herself to think happy thoughts, but they were vague compared to the ugliness that invaded even her prayers. Trucks barreled down dark highways. Red-mouthed dogs hunted in a pack. Silver-sided sharks cruised beneath peacefully lapping waves.

But she'd wakened to the voice of a horse. Had Hoku come home?

Darby threw back the sheet, rolled onto her knees, and peered outside.

No Hoku, but her disappointment was tempered by the surprise of Megan on a bronze-colored horse.

"Get up and put on your boots," the older girl called. "I have a soccer game at noon."

Darby didn't argue. If Megan was out there hollering her intentions, Jonah couldn't have grounded her from riding in search of Hoku.

"Two minutes," Darby yelled back, and even though she made a detour to slip the folded green paper from her book and tuck it carefully into her pocket, she made it.

Megan wore jeans and a baseball cap. She sat so gracefully in the saddle, the horse didn't even have to move for Megan to look like a professional rider.

"You owe me big-time," Megan informed Darby.

"Okay."

"You know I don't ride anymore," Megan began.

"Okay," Darby repeated.

"We're going looking for Hoku because . . ." Megan shrugged. "I'm afraid for your little horse. Besides, I'm a good hostess. And don't say *okay* again."

"All right," Darby said, and though she appreciated Megan's sympathy for Hoku, it only made the filly's danger more real.

"Jonah and Kimo are riding up Sky Mountain. There was a band of horses up there once, and your

filly could have found them. If they're still—"
Megan's head snapped to the side as she noticed Cade
leading Navigator toward them. She muttered something that sounded like, "Of course." Then, in a
normal tone, she said, "Why don't you go grab your
horse, so Cade doesn't have to walk all the way over
here."

Darby hurried to meet Cade. After all, this wasn't
a riding stable where a groom was paid to bring your
horse around. After being out half the night looking
for Hoku, it was great of Cade to saddle and bridle
Navigator for her.

"Thanks so much," Darby said, reaching for
Navigator's reins. Cade just nodded before walking
on, toward Megan.

Navigator nudged Darby with his rust-colored
nose, then rubbed his forehead against her chest.

"Have you been lonely, boy?" she asked the big
gelding, and then, since Jonah was miles away and
couldn't see her, Darby gave Navigator a pat on the
shoulder, before leading him over to Cade and
Megan.

". . . the only person I ever liked calling me
'Mekana' was my dad." Megan practically growled
the words.

"No problem," Cade said. "Just be careful."

He turned, poncho flaring out like a cape. As he
strode past, Darby noticed Cade's blush. His crooked
jaw was set hard as if his teeth were gritted together.

When Darby glanced at Megan for a clue to what had just happened, Megan was sending a poisonous glare after Cade. Catching Darby's stare, Megan took a pair of sunglasses from atop her baseball cap and slid them on.

"Let's go," she said, but her tone warned she wasn't about to answer any questions.

The horse Megan rode was Conch, a grulla Quarter Horse that Jonah was training. Once they'd ridden down the road and turned left, Megan said, "Riding Conch hard was a condition of me being able to take you out this morning. Jonah's still pretty mad at you."

"Right." Darby clipped the word off.

Just as Megan didn't want to talk about Cade, Darby didn't want to talk about Jonah. Half of her blamed him for her foolhardiness. If he hadn't scoffed at her, saying she'd made Hoku worse, she wouldn't have had to prove him wrong. However, the logical half of her brain said no one but her had led Hoku into the night, then lost her.

"Where shall we ride first?" Megan asked.

Between nightmares, Darby had tried to think like her horse. Hoku had probably headed west, just as Kit thought she would, but the filly had learned to stay away from the Zinks' wire. She might head downhill, because the going would be easier. The filly could have gone anywhere, but Darby had decided Hoku would run toward Crimson Vale.

"What if we check out Crimson Vale, since Biscuit went lame before Kit got down in there?" Darby asked.

"Perfect," Megan said. "I know a way in from this side that's not accessible to cars. We can probably get to the waterfall trail and back before it's time for me to get ready. Plus, that's where most of the wild horses are."

"Thanks, Megan," she said, "for, you know, paying attention."

They rode a few more steps before Darby asked, "Is Biscuit yours?"

"Biscuit was my dad's horse. He was training a Crimson Vale horse for me, but she ran off," Megan said, then changed the subject. "If we take the ravine up to the waterfall trail, we'll have a good view of the whole valley."

Darby concentrated on holding her reins the way Jonah had showed her, and balancing on Navigator's back, as they searched for hoofprints.

"Last night's rain has washed out just about everything," Megan said, "but she'd probably go this way, because it smells like other horses. That's my guess."

"That's good enough for me," Darby said lightly, but when she imagined herself as Hoku, searching the night for a hint of home, she knew they were going the right way.

They rode off the road, cross-country, on some

path only Megan and the horses saw. Once, they headed through someone's backyard—judging by the laundry hanging on the line—and another time they picked their way through a grove of trees planted in straight lines like an orchard.

At last, Darby decided Megan had cooled off enough that she could ask, "Does it bother you when Cade calls you"—she'd almost said 'Mekana,' which had to be the Hawaiian version of Megan, but she stopped just in time—"that name, because it reminds you of your dad?"

"It's not the name that bothers me. It's Cade."

"Oh," Darby said, but she knew that couldn't be the end of it. Just as she couldn't play dumb at school, she couldn't deny even a slight friendship. "He's kind of a weird kid, but I like him."

"That's because you don't know what he's capable of. Take the right fork in the path," Megan said over her shoulder.

What he's capable of?

"That sounds like . . ." Darby turned the words over in her mind, then said, "You're thinking of murder or something."

Ahead of her, Megan's spine stiffened and she said, "Or something."

Whoa, Darby warned herself. What did she really know about Cade?

"Careful in here; it's still pretty slippery," Megan said, pointing at the damp patches amid the dozens of red-flowered trees. Then, looking ahead, she asked, "If we stop, can you mount again?"

"Yeah, as long as there's something to use as a mounting block." Darby saw a boulder she could use, if she was careful and Navigator didn't do anything unexpected.

"Good, because this ravine gets steep. We need to double-check our cinches and chest collars, so nobody loses a saddle. That would be so inconvenient, don't you agree?"

Thunder rolled overhead and both girls looked up in surprise.

"Absolutely." Darby laughed, willing to shake off the gloom and suspicion if Megan was.

Still, she wondered if this would be a good time to bring out the green paper she'd folded into her pocket. Megan could help her decipher the letter Jonah had written to her mother.

Darby's hand was in her pocket when rain came pounding down.

"Rain's the price we pay for all this green grass," Megan said as she swung to the ground. "But I could sure stand a day without it." She looked up at Darby. "You know what? There's no reason for you to get down. I can check the cinch and collar with you in the saddle."

"It's no problem," Darby protested, but Megan made a forget-about-it gesture and slipped her hand between Navigator's cinch and belly.

We could be friends, Darby thought, looking down on Megan's quick, kind movements around the horses, *but I'd sure like to know what she has against Cade.*

"Ready," Megan said once she'd checked each horse's gear. She led the way at an easy jog. Conch's hooves splatted on the wet ground. "Lean forward," Megan said as the horses tackled the steepest, slipperiest part of the trail.

When they rested the horses at the top, Darby's heart lurched with eagerness to keep on. She glanced around. Her subconscious mind must have picked up something that made her certain Hoku had stopped here, too.

Darby saw nothing, but her pulse said, *go, go, go.*

Megan stretched tall in the saddle, lifting her hands toward the sky before they rode on. "It'll be slippery going downhill, back to the ranch, but you know, this is lots more fun than I remembered."

Darby heard the smile in Megan's voice and wondered if she'd quit riding because she was busy with school and sports, or for some other reason. Why would she give up horses if she didn't have to?

But she agreed with Megan about the rain. Darby pulled up her collar and held it closed at her throat to keep the water out. It was a losing battle, but the rain hitting her sleeves seemed to run off. Her mom had given her this white shirt because it was supposed to "breathe" in all weather.

Darby was about to ask Megan about hats. If she

stayed for six months, like she was supposed to, she'd need one.

If Jonah let her stay.

If they found Hoku.

Stalled by her thoughts, Darby barely heard Conch snort, but Megan did.

"What is it, boy?" Megan asked, stopping the horse. She laid her hand on the grulla's neck, and followed his gaze into brush bent by the rain. "It's not a boar, is it?"

The fear in Megan's voice and the rustling came at the same time Conch dropped his head to buck.

Before Darby could think what to do, Navigator backed away with dignified disapproval.

Head down and heels up, Conch twisted his body into an impossible hopping corkscrew, but Megan stayed on.

Then, as quickly as the bucking had started, it stopped. Concentrating on her horse, Megan backed the gelding past Navigator. She made the grulla obey a series of commands to turn, to stop and go, then urged him back toward Darby and tightened her hands so he stood.

Red-cheeked and rueful, Megan pulled her cap down firmly, then said, "Gosh, tell me that my last words before Conch went nuts weren't 'This is more fun than I remembered'?"

"I think that was it," Darby said. "You're an amazing rider."

"Not really," Megan said. The trail was flatter now and wide enough that they rode alongside each other.

Something Megan had said had made Darby worry for Hoku. What had it been?

Then Darby remembered. "Did you say something about a boar?" When Megan didn't answer, Darby glanced at her. "What's wrong?"

Megan's face had turned pale. Her right arm curled across her middle as if her stomach hurt, but then dropped away. She shook her head, glanced at her watch, and pointed at the path ahead.

"There's kind of a little cave up there, the only one on this side of the cliffs. Let's get out of this rain for a few minutes before we have to start back, okay?"

Darby didn't want to stop, but Megan's dismay was real. Darby knew the intuition that Hoku was nearby might only be hope.

As they dismounted, Darby realized she wasn't far from where she'd seen the wild horse with the one blue eye.

"I know where we are," Darby blurted. "I stopped here with Kimo, coming from the airport."

"I don't think so," Megan said. "Cars can't get in here."

"But I recognize that." Darby pointed to the black rock teeter-totter she'd used as a landmark. Still, she wondered why she hadn't noticed this shallow cave before.

"Those are remains of altars," Megan said. "They're all over the place. I think you were up higher on the pali—the sea cliffs."

Darby remembered the view. She'd almost become part of it by not watching her feet.

"In here," Megan said, motioning Darby to a rock outcropping. "I'm sorry we haven't seen any sign of Hoku." They crouched under cover, holding their reins while the horses sampled the foliage. "Maybe she's gone home by now."

"I don't think she knows the ranch is home," Darby said. The words hung there as both girls gazed at the falling rain.

Darby tried to summon up mental pictures of all her "homes," but her eyes dropped to the vines outside the stone shelter instead. They sent out runners everywhere, leaves turning and twisting to catch a ray of sun.

Like her mom running from audition to audition, Darby thought wryly, hoping each small change in her appearance or acting style would snare her a role that would catapult her into stardom.

They'd lived eight places since Darby's parents had broken up. Before Pacific Pinnacles, they'd lived in a studio apartment near an old pier. There, she'd learned to swim in the ocean and she'd loved hearing merry-go-round music from the seaside amusement park. Before that, they'd spent a few months in a converted garage in Angelinas. It smelled strongly of cats. One day the curtains over an open window had flapped in and grazed the hot plate. The resulting fire hadn't even set off the smoke alarm, but they'd moved soon after.

The other places were blurry in Darby's memory, but it didn't matter. They moved each time their finances changed.

Now, she thought about Jonah's family—and her mom's, and hers, too, really—living on the ranch for generations.

"Rain's slacking off," Megan said.

The vines had stopped vibrating under raindrops. Darby wondered why the vines stretched green tendrils toward the darkness inside this cave when there was light outside. She thought of the course catalog Megan had brought her and wondered if she'd be in Hawaii long enough to do a science project.

'Iolani Ranch would make a good home if her mom came here to live, too. But she wouldn't, because of Jonah.

I could put up with him, like Mom thought I could, Darby decided, *if it weren't for his unrealistic expectations!*

Megan's boots scuffed. She was about to stand up and go.

Now or never, Darby thought. She pulled the letter from her pocket.

"What's that?" Megan asked.

"Something I hope you can help me understand,"

Darby said. "A letter from Jonah to my mom."

Megan took off her cap and shook it dry. "I won't ask why *you* have it."

"She threw it away," Darby said, as if that excused her prying.

But Megan was apparently too curious to stand on principle. She'd already started reading it.

Darby looked over Megan's shoulder to read the letter again.

Dear Daughter,

You, Darby, and her horse are welcome here and I am grateful for the chance to teach her of her family, her 'aumakua, and horses. You say she is timid, but the picture of her with the pueo-*marked horse shows me sleeping bravery. You must remember that it is the grandparents' right to take as* hanai *the* hiapo, *but we will let Darby herself decide.*

Sincerely,
Jonah

"That word, *'aumakua*, means your family guardians," Megan said, pointing, "like—"

"Owls," Darby interrupted.

"Yeah," Megan said, "and this . . ." She touched the place where Jonah had written *pueo*.

"Means owl," Darby said, then placed her hand over her mouth for a second. "Sorry, I guess I've learned a few things since I've been here, but what is this?" She tapped the last line of Jonah's letter.

"I should make you suffer, for being so rude," Megan joked. Then she drew a deep breath and explained. "It's an old Hawaiian custom for grandparents to adopt the firstborn child. *Hanai* is like adopt, or foster—"

"Like Cade?" Darby asked.

"In this case, it means adoption. The grandparents just kind of expected the parents to hand over the *hiapo*, the firstborn. And that's you, right? You don't have any older brothers or sisters?"

Darby shook her head, feeling dizzy.

Just hand her over? Is that what Jonah thought this was about?

"So, he didn't ask me to Hawaii so he could get his hands on Hoku," Darby mumbled.

"You didn't really think that, did you?" Megan asked. "Jonah has plenty of horses. You know, those four-legged animals roaming all over the—"

"Stop," Darby told her.

"And if you haven't noticed, he's not real thrilled with *wild* horses. He'll do whatever it takes to keep them away from his Quarter Horses. Bloodlines are important."

The rain had stopped, but Darby still sat staring, until Megan interrupted her thoughts.

"There's one thing you can be thankful for," Megan offered. She looked around cautiously and whispered, "At least your family guardian's not a rock."

"A rock? Your *'aumakua* is a *rock*? What does it do to protect you, fall on people?"

"Nope, my *'aumakua* is *honu*, the sea turtle," Megan said, "but—"

Megan broke off, shaking her head, and Darby knew she was probably jumping to conclusions when she imagined Megan had been about to warn her that mocking an *'aumakua* was risky business.

Chapter 21

Darby climbed onto Navigator from a boulder. The black rock slab would have made a perfect mounting block, but since Megan had told her it might be an ancient altar, there was no way she'd climb on it.

They'd only ridden a few steps when Darby hesitated. She couldn't remember the name of that game where you tried to find something while people shouted "warmer" as you got near it and "colder" as you turned the wrong way. But her instincts had been shouting "hotter" all the way up here, and suddenly they were screaming, "On fire!"

Megan rode on. As Darby stared after her, she knew what she was feeling didn't make sense. This wasn't an instinct like animals had, just a mix of dreams and longing.

Then Darby heard something familiar. It sounded a lot like a hoot.

Gooseflesh crawled from her scalp down her arms.

"What kind of tree is that? The one with the red flowers?" she asked Megan.

"Ohia," Megan said without looking.

"Ohia," Darby echoed, but her eyes focused on the owl perched in the red-flowered tree. "What's that owl doing out in broad daylight?"

Even now, Megan barely glanced at it. "Probably hunting. I see them in the fields sometimes. Personally, I just think they hunt at night a lot because they have the advantage over animals that don't see in the dark as well as they do."

Megan's remark made perfect sense, but Darby couldn't stop studying the owl. In the light, she saw its rounded wings and eyes as yellow as lemon drops.

It was unlikely that this was the same owl that lived near Hoku's ranch corral. Owls had territories, didn't they? Darby had always considered herself levelheaded, and she'd nearly talked herself out of viewing this bird as an omen, when it launched itself from the tree, glided between her and Megan, then disappeared into the trees.

"Is it . . ."—Darby searched her vocabulary for a word that didn't sound superstitious—"*customary* for an owl to do that?"

"I'm no owl expert," Megan said.

"Okay then, if an owl does that, flies across your path, is it warning you to stay where you are?"

Darby weighed the rules she'd grown up with versus superstition. But what if it wasn't superstition? What if ancient Hawaiians had lived so close to the natural world, they understood the wing ruffling and head tilting language of owls?

Just suppose the owl had hooted at her because she wasn't supposed to leave Crimson Vale until she'd removed an intruder on the owl's territory — Hoku?

Megan considered her with such a pitying look, Darby tried to sound casual.

"Hey, you know what? I'm going to stay up here and look around for a little while, just check out the area, see what I can see. . . ."

"Sometimes an owl is just an owl, Darby." Megan shrugged.

"Sure, but if I were Hoku, I'd head for other wild horses. And this is where they hang out, right? If I sit here quietly, Hoku might come to me. We were doing really well together before I was stupid enough to let her run away."

"Do you know what Jonah would do if I left you up here alone? Can you even find your way back to the ranch?"

"Well . . ." Darby looked at the dense foliage. All the trees and bushes looked so much the same.

Except the red-flowered ohia.

"Do you know which path leads to the road and which way to turn if you do happen to find it?" Megan shook her head. "Not to be mean, but Darby, you thought you were at the outlook a thousand feet *up* from here."

When you were used to living your life as someone smart, it felt awful to be dumb, Darby thought.

"Navigator can find his way home," she said, though her hope of winning was fading.

"No way."

"I've thought of a compromise," Darby said.

"'No way' doesn't leave room for negotiation, girl," Megan said.

"I have the cell phone—"

"Like it would work here," Megan snapped.

"It will work as a timer. I'll watch you ride out, then stay here for thirty minutes and sit quietly. If Hoku comes to me, I'll lead her back to the ranch. If she doesn't, Navigator will try to catch up with Conch."

"Thirty minutes," Megan repeated, then pretended to strike her forehead. "No. Why am I even considering it?"

Megan closed her eyes as if blocking out Darby's face helped her to concentrate.

Then, Megan asked, "If—and this is a big if—I agreed to stay thirty more minutes with you, where would you look for her?"

"Where I was with Kimo, where I saw a wild horse."

"It would take hours to get up there. We came in from the opposite side of the valley," Megan pointed out.

Grab this chance, Darby told herself. Thirty minutes of searching was better than nothing.

Past the dripping of rain-washed leaves and the calling of birds, Darby heard the rolling of ocean waves, faint and far off as the sound inside a shell. Suddenly, the splash from her dream resounded in her mind.

"Is there a place we can see the beach from here?" Darby asked. "The beach might remind Hoku of Nevada's *playa*. It's a desert area that was the bottom of an ancient lake," she explained when Megan looked confused. "In Spanish, *playa* means 'beach.' I know it's a long shot—"

"What it is, is a long *fall*," Megan said, "but I'll show you."

They dismounted and tied up the horses. As they walked through a tunnel of greenery, the rush of waves grew louder. The vegetation thinned, the rock underfoot was smooth, and suddenly they'd reached the sea cliffs that plummeted down to the Pacific Ocean.

Megan's arm snapped out to bar Darby from walking too near the edge.

"Wow, this makes me understand why people told

Christopher Columbus he could sail off the edge of the world," Darby said. She wasn't so sure they weren't right.

"Right below us, there's just a little cove with a beach, but around that lava spit—that thing like a black rock finger pointing out to sea?—there's a smooth, wide shore called Night Digger Point Beach. We just can't see it from here," Megan said. She drew a deep breath of sea air.

"I'm going to look down, but I won't move my feet," Darby said. Even knowing she'd be dizzied by the height, she had to do it.

First she saw her boots. Past them, a few wisps of hardy sea grass blew toward her. She looked a bit farther, and saw it wasn't really a sheer drop to the waves. A lava flow had cooled with bubbles, scoops, and arches. She looked for a path a horse could take, but hooves couldn't grip rock.

"The tide's coming in, so—" Megan gasped, then backed away from the edge.

What had Megan seen? Good sense told Darby to back away, but curiosity made her lean from the waist to look where Megan had.

Hoku stood on a white crescent of beach, staring out to sea.

"Come on, we'll ride back to the ranch and Jonah can call someone with a boat," Megan said. "They used to lead cattle from boats all the time. . . ."

Darby didn't listen. There had to be a way down

there. The filly had to be lonely enough to allow herself to be led.

But where could she lead her?

Looking right, there was nothing except the black lava spit, dividing the cove from open ocean.

Looking left, she saw a solid rock wall.

How had the filly gotten down there? Had Hoku swum to the beach from somewhere else?

It didn't matter. Turquoise water lapped around Hoku's hooves. The filly struck at it. Judging from the seaweed clinging to the rock face below, the water level in that cove could rise as high as Hoku's head.

"If only we had a rope," Darby cried. "Kimo told me people carrying the bodies of royalty to their burial caves were lowered on ropes, and you're strong enough to lower me, I bet."

"Did he also tell you they died?" Megan demanded.

"They killed themselves," Darby corrected. "I'm not going to do that."

Not on purpose, anyway, she amended silently.

"Darby, we're wasting time," Megan said. "We've got to get Jonah or my —"

"You said there's a beach on the other side of that spit," Darby interrupted, mind spinning. "I'm a really good swimmer. If Hoku would —"

Darby stopped when she saw Hoku trotting from one edge of her natural corral to the other, her steps light and nervous. The filly didn't know the ocean, but she knew pursuit. Water was coming after her, drawing closer every second. Cold water nipped at her heels like a coyote.

"You might be a good swimmer, but not here. There are sharks and dangerous currents," Megan insisted, then she grabbed Darby's wrist. Her fingers reached all the way around it.

Darby felt absolutely scrawny when she looked at Megan's strong fingers holding her captive, but she wouldn't give up.

"You're an athlete," Darby said calmly. "I'm sure you can drag me away from here if you decide that's what you need to do. But Hoku will drown if I don't help her swim around the spit to the other beach."

"She might swim on her own," Megan said.

"But she probably won't, and I have a better chance of climbing down than she does of climbing up. I know people have gone down there. We came through that tunnel in the foliage, and there was a faint path."

"Grave robbers," Megan said.

"Grave robbers?" Darby repeated, but she was stalling.

Megan's fingers had loosened. Darby spotted a shelf of rock about six feet below them. She could drop to it.

In a defense-against-muggers magazine article, she'd read that if a bad guy grabbed your arm, you were supposed to jerk toward the weakest part of his grip, where the fingertips met.

"Those burial caves are easier to reach if you go across from here and back up, and they're filled with artifacts. Cursed, they say, but valuable." A dark furrow appeared between Megan's brows. "So, yeah, there must be a way down. Let me think."

A soaring neigh cut through the wave's thunder.

"She sees me!" Darby cried, then jerked her wrist loose from Megan's grasp and jumped.

"You are so dead!" Megan screamed from just over Darby's head.

Her echoing voice made Darby shudder, but she was too busy searching for a trail to give in to worry.

"I'm coming down there and when I get my hands on you, you'll be so sorry!" Megan yelled.

It wasn't hard going, but Darby was concentrating on the placement of each step, so it took a few seconds for Megan's words to sink in.

"No!" she shouted upward. "She'll run from you!"

"Then what am I supposed to do?" Megan's voice seemed to tremble, but it could have been that Darby heard it through waves and rushing sea wind. "This is what I get for being nice to you!" she shouted, but her voice was fainter.

Darby looked up. Megan had vanished from the cliff top.

Okay, I'm alone, Darby thought. She sat and tugged off her boots. Bare feet would grip the rocks better.

"I'm not taking the blame for this." Megan's voice

came to Darby so faintly, she wouldn't have heard the last bit except that it hung on the wind. "You're cra-zy!"

The rocks burned the bottoms of Darby's feet. Once, she came to a place where there was a strange scatter of boulders as big as her head and had to backtrack up the face of the pali, then start down again. But those were her only complaints.

The climb was wild and beautiful. A tree covered with purple flowers clung to a sandy spot amid all the sheer stone, surrounded by a profusion of ferns.

Sudden sea spray soaked Darby as she stepped over stringy shreds of bark, afraid she'd ensnare herself and trip.

Another worried neigh floated to her, followed by snorts of fear.

"I'm coming, baby!" Darby yelled, and then, because she'd looked down at Hoku instead of her footing, something brown looped over her instep.

Snake. Primal fear overcame knowledge for a second and she kicked to get free. Not a snake but tiny white flowers caused her to trip and pitch forward. Then the stem snapped and Darby was falling.

Glimpses of ocean, ferns, rocks as holey as Swiss cheese, and Jonah's cell phone arcing in a silver parabola all tilted together in a crazy collage. Her chin struck a lava edge that was sharp as a knife. She grabbed the ledge with both hands and her body jerked to a stop.

Her feet swung in the air.

Panting, trying to dredge up breath from deep in her lungs, Darby willed her hands to stop shaking. Telling them to stop bleeding probably wouldn't work, but she held on tight enough that she could rest her chin on her shoulder and look back.

Just as before, she saw sun diamonds glinting on teal-blue waves, but this time she saw Hoku, too. The filly held her head high and her ears pricked toward Darby.

Darby tightened her grip. She couldn't fail now.

Her eyes burned as she rolled them to see the closest footing she could reach.

The sight below her was good. If she dropped a mere foot, she'd almost be down. A circling flock of birds investigated her as she straightened her elbows, hung, then dropped onto a shelf of rock.

She turned slowly, then climbed down, skirting tide pools and slippery clumps of kelp until she reached the beach.

She staggered a few feet and closed her eyes.

Sand prickled on her toes. Waves roared, then whispered as they sneaked ashore. Seabirds squealed overhead, and suddenly the red tracery of veins on the inside of her eyelids went dark.

Darby opened her eyes just as Hoku's nose touched hers. The filly jerked back, proving her neck was just fine.

"I used to lead a normal life," she told the mustang, but Hoku blew a disbelieving snort.

The tide kept rolling in. Their lives were at stake, but Darby was mesmerized by the sight of the filly she thought she'd lost.

A magical sea horse sculpted of ivory and gold, Hoku stood silhouetted against the ocean. She lowered her head and gazed at Darby through her forelock.

What if I don't know how to be your leader? Darby thought. But Hoku was looking to her, the bringer-of-hay, for help, and Darby had one good idea.

Swimming was something she did well. Getting Hoku to follow would be the hard part. But together they *would* reach that beach on the far side of the spit.

Darby measured the distance between herself and her horse. She stood close enough to reach the leather string that still dangled from Hoku's halter. She raised her arm, held it still for an endless minute until Hoku lost interest, then closed her thumb and forefinger in a pinching grip.

The filly started backward, out of reach, heels splashing into the waves.

"No big deal, girl," Darby cooed, trying to convince the filly she'd overreacted. "I won't lead you, then. We'll just go swimming."

Darby tried not to think of sharks, though she remembered reading an interview with a marine biologist who'd estimated that there was one shark for each hundred people in the Hawaiian islands. Or maybe that was Australia.

She wasn't hurt, just a little scuffed up, but her chin was bleeding and so were her hands. Blood drifted through the water like smoke, and sharks smelled it.

So, she could stay here and drown in this little cove with Hoku, or risk being eaten alive. Both were more appealing than her third choice: abandoning her horse.

Sure, she could climb back up the rock face she'd just descended. Navigator might still be up there, and Megan, too, and no one—not Cathy, Kimo, Kit, and definitely not Jonah—would be the least bit surprised she'd been too scared to save Hoku's life. And they wouldn't care. They'd probably treat her the same as they'd been treating her.

But I care, Darby thought. *It's time to stop thinking and start swimming*.

Darby waded into the cove, calling, "C'mon, girl."

Warm waves, soft with foam from hammering over a barricade of rocks, curled around Darby's knees, then her thighs. Her toes gripped sand. She took a breath and pushed off, arrowing into the water. Surfacing, she shook back her wet, black hair and struck out, swimming.

Beneath one arm, she glimpsed Hoku trotting up and down the tiny beach.

She stopped, treading water, and shouted, "Come

on, girl. You can do it!"

Hoku squealed, tossed her golden mane, then reared in frustration, demanding Darby's return.

I'm not going back, Darby thought, and this time her determination wasn't about proving herself to Jonah. She might not know a lot about horses, but she knew about swimming.

And drowning. She could no longer see Hoku's hooves. The filly jerked her knees high, but she wasn't prancing. She wanted to break away from the rising water.

Darby's hands sculled across the surface of the water. How could she tell the filly that she must plunge into the sea before she could escape it?

I can't explain, Darby realized. *She's got to trust me, even if she doesn't know why.*

Darby floated up. Each wave passing her was headed for Hoku.

"We're in the same herd, sweetie," Darby yelled, cupping one hand around her mouth so that Hoku could hear her voice over the waves, "but I'm the lead mare."

I have to show her I mean it, Darby thought. Arms trembling, she turned her back on Hoku and kept swimming.

A warm current flowed around her.

Not a shark, please, she begged, and it wasn't.

Her toes grazed a sun-warmed shelf of rock. Lava

had flowed out here and cooled underwater, she thought, but she only stood on it for a second, because here came Hoku swimming after her, proud chest raising a frill of foam.

She had to lead the filly into deeper water.

Gasping on a sudden mouthful of saltwater, Darby coughed, dove, then stroked and kicked with all her strength until she reached the point of the lava spit.

A glance back showed Darby that Hoku was catching up with her.

Ahead . . .

Darby pulled at the waves with one arm and rubbed water beads from her eyelashes with the other, but she wasn't imagining it.

There it was, a swathe of white beach.

Hoku huffed and glided closer, swimming smoothly as if Nevada mustangs did this all the time.

"C'mon, baby. Keep coming!"

Elation gave Darby energy, but her strong strokes didn't bring her closer to the beach.

She concentrated on form, making mighty kicks, pressing her fingers together, but the beach shrank as she moved farther out to sea.

Dangerous currents, Megan had warned, but Darby knew what to do in riptides and fluky waves. Swim parallel to the beach. Still, each bullying wave withdrawing from the beach pushed her head under.

Spitting out a mouthful of water, she kept calling encouragement to Hoku.

"My little sea horse," she managed.

What would happen when Megan brought help to the wrong place? They'd look just on the other side of the spit, at the first patch of beach where she and Hoku should have come ashore.

Was she leading Hoku to some whirlpool of death made by waterfalls pounding into the surf? Would a floating raft of uprooted palm trees beat and break her bones?

Shake it off, Darby told herself. A search party led by Jonah wouldn't give up. They'd keep looking until they found hoofprints in the sand where she and Hoku had come ashore.

Don't stop talking to Hoku.

"Horse paddle is so much cooler than dog paddle, yeah?" she screeched with what felt like her last calorie of energy.

Darby's legs went limp, sagging down from the surface. A crisp TV image of how much like seals swimmers looked to sharks floating below took form in her mind.

When something trailed over her sculling fingers, Darby snatched her hand back against her chest.

But it was only Hoku's tail. The filly swam past, head lurching forward with each swimming stride.

Did she dare grab that golden tail and let Hoku

tow her through the water? Was it Hoku's turn to rescue her?

Darby decided it was. After flashing her a single look of astonishment, Hoku kept swimming.

Chapter 22

She didn't remember Hoku dragging her onto the beach, but when Darby regained consciousness, she lay on her back. She felt warm sand beneath her. Above, she saw Hoku's belly. The filly stood four-square over her, like a golden tent with four posts.

Water dripped off the horse onto her face. Darby tensed at her vulnerable position. But when Hoku looked backward, between her front legs, chewing some kind of sea grass, she looked so comical that Darby laughed.

"There's hay at the ranch," she promised the filly, and Hoku walked forward a few steps so that Darby could get up.

The problem with putting your faith in owls,

Darby thought with bleary logic, was that you didn't plan much. She had no food or water. She'd climbed a long way down, and been swept miles from where she'd left Megan. Should she stay here and wait, or start for the ranch?

Exertion and asthma convinced her to stay put until she recovered her strength. Amazed that her medicine had remained stuck in her pocket, Darby used her inhaler, then choked. Her throat was sore from saltwater. The sting of medicine made her cough so much she was afraid Hoku would bolt.

But the filly was hungry. The salty grass was enough to make her stay, and her neck must be nearly healed, because she grazed without stopping.

Darby wished for Jonah's cell phone. She remembered the sound of it banging a boulder, then disappearing between the rocks, rattling as it fell.

If she'd had it, she could have called the ranch or 911, but she didn't have the cell phone and she hadn't seen or heard a single searcher. So, when the sun reached a position she guessed was about three o'clock in the afternoon, Darby decided it was time to go.

"We'd better start walking," she told Hoku as the filly blinked out of a nap. "And do you know why we're really glad this is the smallest inhabited island in Hawaii? Because we want to reach the ranch before dark."

For about half an hour, Darby and Hoku hiked side by side. They'd left the beach and cliff behind and a forest lay ahead. Darby wanted to reach for the leather string still dangling from her filly's halter, but she didn't want the mustang to shy and run away.

Once, Darby stopped. She thought she'd heard something like a motorcycle or jet ski. She stood listening, and Hoku did, too.

Darby held her breath, but she didn't hear anyone calling her name. When Hoku walked on, Darby went with her.

They plodded on for a long time. Darby saw no wild horses and signs of human habitation, except for a path, so she followed it.

Her sore feet were soothed by red mud. She didn't know when sand had given way to dirt, then mud, and she didn't care.

"Wow, does that feel as good on your hooves as it does on my feet?" Darby asked Hoku.

Then she realized each time she spoke, Hoku had edged closer to her.

"Just like that day in the snow, right, girl?" Darby asked in a singsong voice that made the filly's ears prick toward her. "If I keep talking, maybe you'll follow me all the way back to your cozy corral, where I'll give you all the hay you can eat!"

A pair of birds burst from a clump of greenery and Darby's heart pounded hard, thinking of the black boar Megan had mentioned. If the creature decided to charge, she wouldn't have a chance.

But she wouldn't give in without a fight.

Darby gathered stones, carrying them in a pouch made by holding the hem of her T-shirt. And she started watching the woods around her for a fallen branch that she could use as a club.

As her attention wandered, so did Hoku.

Darby chattered to lure her horse back.

"How close are we to the ranch? That's what I asked Kimo on that first day before we came to get you," Darby told Hoku, "and he said, 'Twenty minutes or so,' but he meant in a truck. It would be cool if you decided you could give me a ride, but don't think I'm not grateful you're following instead of leading."

As if she'd understood those last words, Hoku walked a bit faster. Darby lengthened her stride even though she was staring around in wonder.

"How did we walk into my dream?" she asked Hoku. "With all these vines and red mud squishing up between my toes . . ."

But it wasn't a restful dream. The sky was turning dark and this wasn't the path she'd taken with Megan. She was lost.

It looked something like Pearl Pasture. Darby stood trying to figure out where she was, wishing she had an animal's sense of smell that would tell her if horses or cattle were nearby.

As Darby concentrated, Hoku moved past her and broke into a trot.

Oh, no. Darby didn't take off after her. If she ran,

the filly could think they were playing a game—that wonderful horse game called Stampede.

But she couldn't let Hoku get away.

Scarlet blooms of lehua whipped Darby's hair. Though the filly ducked, a few flowers caught in her mane as she flashed past.

The jungle canopy blocked out much of the graying light; vegetation squeezed close, leaving a single-file passageway. Hoku moved out of sight.

Each time Darby turned a corner, she hoped she'd see her horse. She didn't, but twice she heard the plop of Hoku's hooves, so she rushed on.

Darby came upon Hoku when the filly stopped to drink from a puddle.

Reflected stars danced on its surface and Darby looked up through a hole between branches into the night sky.

"Stars are the eyes of heaven. That's what Jonah told me, Hoku."

The filly went on drinking as if she didn't notice Darby's fingers closing on the leather string to her halter.

"I'm thirsty myself," Darby complained. "But a person can get sick drinking strange water."

When Hoku glanced up with droplets dripping from her chin, Darby said, "Don't worry. I'm sure you have a much stronger system than I do."

But the filly had drunk her fill. Now she considered the leather string connecting her to Darby.

"You know how to do this," she assured Hoku.

Holding her breath, Darby took a confident step past the sorrel.

"Let's go," she said, and Hoku followed.

Darby was already smiling when she made out an abandoned corral. They were getting closer to the ranch. Or at least some kind of civilization.

The world had darkened to shades of ash and charcoal. As rain pattered down, Darby smelled flowers bowing under the drops. Plants shaped like inside-out umbrellas nodded as if hinting that she and Hoku were on the right path.

Hoku didn't seem to notice the rain. She held her head high and snorted when the trail widened and sloped downward.

Darby's world shrank to this small bit of forest. She'd never noticed that raindrops striking leaves of various sizes, thicknesses, and shapes made different sounds.

Now, she heard the music of the leaves.

All at once, the forest opened and Darby knew the cottage from her dream sat in the clearing. If she turned toward it, a door would open and help would be offered.

She didn't do it.

"Call me crazy," Darby told Hoku, "but we've made it this far alone and I . . ."

Even to the filly, she couldn't explain.

She'd braved falls, drowning, sharks, and boars to

bring her horse to safety. She wasn't about to beg for help now. And who knew what was really in that cottage, if it existed at all.

Hoku halted. She stood trembling, staring at a dark figure.

It spoke.

"Rumor says there's a new horse charmer on Wild Horse Island."

Darby's breath caught in her throat. She couldn't see the expression on her grandfather's face, but she knew what Hoku was feeling.

A living thing had materialized in front of them, and it was a *man*.

Darby touched the filly's shoulder and whispered to her. In a few seconds, Hoku's breathing slowed. So did Darby's.

She replayed the tone of Jonah's words. He was joking.

"Hoku insists I speak horse, so we're just learning to talk to each other," Darby said, and she was smiling.

"Well, everyone's out looking for you. You sure took the long way home."

Jonah punctuated the sentence with a short laugh, and Darby said, "But I made it."

"You did," Jonah agreed, and she pictured the pleased crinkling at the corner of his eyes.

Jonah turned to lead the way home, but Darby didn't follow right away.

Hoku crowded close behind her, then hung her head over Darby's right shoulder.

Darby held her breath, not daring to swallow or even breathe. The mustang filly was rubbing her mane against Darby's wet black hair, as if they were sisters.

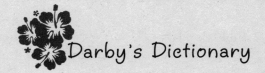

Darby's Dictionary

In case anybody reads this besides me, which it's too late to tell you not to do if you've gotten this far, I know this isn't a real dictionary. For one thing, it's not all correct, and for another, it's not alphabetized because I'm just adding things as I hear them. Besides, this dictionary is just to help me remember. Even though I'm pretty self-conscious about pronouncing Hawaiian words, it seems to me if I live here (and since I'm part Hawaiian), I should at least try to say things right.

'aumakua — OW MA KOO AH — these are family guardians from ancient times. I think ancestors are supposed to come back and look out for their family members. Our 'aumakua are owls and Megan's is a sea turtle.

hanai — HA NYE E — a foster or adopted child, like Cade is Jonah's, but I don't know if it's permanent

'iolani — EE OH LAWN EE — this is a hawk that brings messages from the gods, but Jonah has it painted on his trucks as an owl bursting through the clouds

hiapo — HIGH AH PO — a firstborn child, like me, and it's apparently tradition for grandparents, if they feel like it, to just take hiapo to raise!

hoku — HO COO — star

ali'i — AH LEE EE — royalty, but it includes chiefs besides queens and kings and people like that

pupule — POO POO LAY — crazy

paniolo — PAW KNEE OH LOW — cowboy or cowgirl

lanai — LAH NA E — this is like a balcony or veranda. Sun House's is more like a long balcony with a view of the pastures.

luna — LOU NUH — a boss or top guy, like Jonah's stallion

pueo — POO AY OH — an owl, our family guardian. The very coolest thing is that one lives in the tree next to Hoku's corral.

pau — POW — finished, like Kimo is always asking, "You pau?" to see if I'm done working with Hoku or shoveling up after the horses

pali — PAW LEE — cliffs

ohia — OH HE UH — a tree like the one next to Hoku's corral

lei — LAY E — necklace of flowers. I thought they were pronounced LAY, but Hawaiians add another sound. I also thought leis were sappy touristy things, but getting one is a real honor, from the right people.

luahala — LOO AH HA LA — some kind of leaf in shades of brown, used to make paniolo hats like Cade's. I guess they're really expensive.

<u>kapu</u> — KAH POO — forbidden, a taboo

<u>tutu</u> — TOO TOO — great-grandmother

<u>menehune</u> — MEN AY WHO NAY — little people

<u>honu</u> — HO NEW — sea turtle

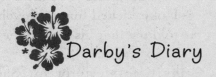

Darby's Diary

<u>Ellen Kealoha Carter</u>—my mom, and since she's responsible for me being in Hawaii, I'm putting her first. Also I miss her. My mom is a beautiful and talented actress, but she hasn't had her big break yet. Her job in Tahiti might be it, which is sort of ironic because she's playing a Hawaiian for the first time and she swore she'd never return to Hawaii. And here I am. I get the feeling she had huge fights with her dad, Jonah, but she doesn't hate Hawaii.

<u>Cade</u>—fifteen or so, he's Jonah's adopted son. Jonah's been teaching him all about being a paniolo. I thought he was Hawaiian, but when he took off his hat he had blond hair—in a braid! Like old-time

vaqueros—weird! He doesn't go to school, just takes his classes by correspondence through the mail. He wears this poncho that's almost black it's such a dark green, and he blends in with the forest. Kind of creepy the way he just appears out there. Not counting Kit, Cade might be the best rider on the ranch.

Hoku kicked him in the chest. I wish she hadn't. He told me that his stepfather beat him all the time.

Cathy Kato—forty or so? She's the ranch manager and, really, the only one who seems to manage Jonah. She's Megan's mom and the widow of a paniolo, Ben. She has messy blond-brown hair to her chin, and she's a good cook, but she doesn't think so. It's like she's just pulling herself back together after Ben's death.

I get the feeling she used to do something with advertising or public relations on the mainland.

Jonah Kaniela Kealoha—my grandfather could fill this whole notebook. Basically, though, he's harsh/nice, serious/funny, full of legends and stories about magic, but real down-to-earth. He's amazing with horses, which is why they call him the Horse Charmer. He's not that tall, maybe 5'8", with black hair that's getting gray, and one of his fingers is still kinked where it was broken by a teacher because he spoke Hawaiian in class! I don't like his "don't touch the horses unless they're working for you" theory, but it totally works. I need to figure out why.

Kimo—he's so nice! I guess he's about twenty-five, Hawaiian, and he's just this sturdy, square, friendly guy. He drives in every morning from his house over by Crimson Vale, and even though he's late a lot, I've never seen anyone work so hard.

Kit Ely—the ranch foreman, the boss, next to Jonah. He's Sam's friend Jake's brother and a real buckaroo. He's about 5'10" with black hair. He's half Shoshone, but he could be mistaken for Hawaiian, if he wasn't always promising to whip up a batch of Nevada chili and stuff like that. And he wears a totally un-Hawaiian leather string with brown-streaked turquoise stones around his neck. He got to be fore-man through his rodeo friend Pani (Ben's buddy?). Kit's left wrist got pulverized in a rodeo fall. He's still amazing with horses, though.

Megan Kato—Cathy's fifteen-year-old daughter, a super athlete with long reddish-black hair. She's beau-tiful and popular and I doubt she'd be my friend if we just met at school. Maybe, though, because she's nice at heart. She half makes fun of Hawaiian legends, then turns around and acts really serious about them. She can't stand Cade and he always blushes around her.

The Zinks—they live on the land next to Jonah. They have barbed-wire fences and their name doesn't sound Hawaiian, but that's all I know.

<u>Tutu</u>—my great-grandmother, but I haven't met her yet. I get the feeling she lives out in the rain forest like a medicine woman or something.

❧ ANIMALS! ❧

<u>Hoku</u>—my wonderful sorrel filly! She's about two and a half years old, a full sister to the Phantom, and boy, does she show it! She's fierce (hates men) but smart, and a one-girl (ME!) horse for sure. She is definitely a herd-girl, and when it comes to choosing between me and other horses, it's a real toss-up. Not that I blame her. She's run free for a long time, and I don't want to take away what makes her special.

She loves hay, but she's really HEAD-SHY due to Shan Stonerow's early "training," which, according to Sam, was beating her.

Hoku means "star." Her dam is Princess Kitty, but her sire is a mustang named Smoke and he's mustang all the way back to a "white renegade with murder in his eye" (Mrs. Allen).

<u>Navigator</u>—my riding horse is a big, heavy Quarter Horse that reminds me of a knight's charger. He has Three Bars breeding (that's a big deal), but when he picked me, Jonah let him keep me! He's black with rusty rings around his eyes and a rusty muzzle. (Even though he looks black, the proper description is

brown, they tell me.) He can find his way home from any place on the island. He's sweet, but no pushover. Just when I think he's sort of a safety net for my beginning riding skills, he tests me.

Joker — Cade's Appaloosa gelding is gray splattered with black spots and has a black mane and tail. He climbs like a mountain goat and always looks like he's having a good time. I think he and Cade have a history, maybe Jonah took them in together?

Biscuit — buckskin gelding, one of Ben's horses, a dependable cowpony. Kit rides him a lot.

Hula Girl — chestnut cutter

Blue Ginger — blue roan mare with tan foal

Honolulu Lulu — bay mare

Tail Afire (Koko) — fudge brown mare with silver mane and tail

Blue Moon — Blue Ginger's baby

Moonfire — Tail Afire's baby

Black Cat — Lady Wong's black foal

<u>Luna Dancer</u>—Hula Girl's bay baby

<u>Honolulu Half Moon</u>

<u>Conch</u>—grulla cowpony, gelding, needs work. Megan rides him sometimes.

<u>Kona</u>—big gray, Jonah's cow horse

<u>Luna</u>—beautiful, full-maned bay stallion is king of 'Iolani Ranch. He and Jonah seem to have a bond.

<u>Lady Wong</u>—dappled gray mare and Kona's dam. Her current foal is Black Cat.

<u>Australian shepherds</u>—pack of five and I have to learn their names!

<u>Pipsqueak/Pip</u>—little, shaggy, white dog that runs with the big dogs, belongs to Megan and Cathy

❧ PLACES ❧

<u>Lehua High School</u>—the school Megan goes to and I will, too. School colors are red and gold.

<u>Crimson Vale</u>—it's an amazing and magical place,

and once I learn my way around, I bet I'll love it. It's like a maze, though. Here's what I know: from town you can go through the valley or take the ridge road—valley has lily pads, waterfalls, wild horses, and rainbows. The ridge route (Pali?) has sweeping turns that almost made me sick. There are black rock teeter-totter-looking things that are really ancient altars and a SUDDEN drop-off down to a white sand beach. Hawaiian royalty are supposedly buried in the cliffs.

<u>Moku Lio Hihiu</u>—Wild Horse Island, of course!

<u>Mountain to the Sky</u>—sometimes just called Sky Mountain. Goes up to 5,000 feet, sometimes gets snow, and Megan said there used to be wild horses there.

<u>The Two Sisters</u>—cone-shaped "mountains." A borderline between them divides Jonah's land from his sister's—my aunt, but I haven't met her. One of them is an active volcano. Kind of scary.

<u>Sun House</u>—our family place. They call it plantation style, but it's like sugar plantation, not Southern mansion. It has an incredible lanai that overlooks pastures all the way to Mountain to the Sky and Two Sisters. Upstairs is this little apartment Jonah built for my mom, but she's never lived in it.

<u>Hapuna</u>—biggest town on island, has airport, flag-pole, public and private schools, etc., palm trees, and coconut trees

<u>ʻIolani Ranch</u>—our home ranch. 2,000 acres, the most beautiful place in the world.

❧ ON THE RANCH, THERE ARE ❧
PASTURES WITH NAMES LIKE:

<u>Sugar Mill</u> and <u>Upper Sugar Mill</u>—for cattle

<u>Two Sisters</u>—for young horses, one- and two-year-olds they pretty much leave alone

<u>Flatland</u>—mares and foals

<u>Pearl Pasture</u>—borders the rain forest, mostly two- and three-year-olds in training

<u>Borderlands</u>—saddle herd and Luna's compound

I guess I should also add me . . .

<u>Darby Leilani Kealoha Carter</u>—I love horses more than anything, but books come in second. I'm thir-

teen, and one-quarter Hawaiian, with blue eyes and black hair down to about the middle of my back. On a good day, my hair is my best feature. I'm still kind of skinny, but I don't look as sickly as I did before I moved here. I think Hawaii's curing my asthma. Fingers crossed.

I have no idea what I did to land on Wild Horse Island, but I want to stay here forever.

Darby and Hoku's adventures continue in . . .

THE SHINING STALLION

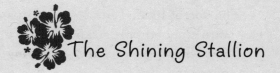 The Shining Stallion

The girl and horse stood nose-to-nose.

Tradewinds swirled the scents of trees and cinnamon red dirt around them. Truck tires crunched on the rough road to 'Iolani Ranch, a goat's bleat mixed with birdsong, and the harsh neigh of a stallion rang out from a distant pasture.

But the girl only noticed her horse's hay-sweet breath and the flick of her flattened ears. Darby smiled at Hoku's determination to win their stare-off.

She'd named the filly Hoku, Hawaiian for "star," after the white marking on her chest, but Darby Carter couldn't help comparing the young horse to something else.

Nitroglycerine, Darby thought as she stepped toward her golden-red filly. One wrong move could make that chemical explode.

Darby scuffed her boots in the dirt. She couldn't move any closer without ramming into the filly, but Hoku didn't know that.

The sorrel braced her legs and tossed her mane. Her stare stabbed past strands of ivory forelock.

Friendship was one thing. Giving into a halter was something else.

Hoku would never be truly tame. Haltering her mustang was about as safe as playing with explosives.

"Hey, good girl, don't look so worried," Darby said.

Hoku vibrated with a silent nicker and her head rose an inch. For a second, Darby felt as if they were the only two creatures on the island, but then Hoku glanced over Darby's shoulder, through the corral rails, and glared at their audience.

"Stay close."

Darby didn't turn at Cade's voice. His eyes tracked her moves, but he wasn't adding up her mistakes. He was keeping her under surveillance, for her own good.

Not that Cade and everyone else on 'Iolani Ranch thought she was insane, but she'd understand if they did. To say she'd made a few big mistakes last week was an understatement. She'd given new meaning to the term "horse crazy."

"But I've learned my lesson, haven't I, pretty girl," Darby said.

Hoku's eyes widened as Darby sauntered around to her left side, but she only looked curious.

Darby and Cade had been talking since dawn about how to halter her head-shy filly. Staying close, without doing anything Hoku found scary, was the first step.

Once, a man had tried to beat the filly's wild-horse-wariness out of her. It hadn't worked. Hoku's spirit matched her fire-gold coat. She hated men and she didn't like anyone, even Darby, touching her head.

"Exhale," Darby whispered to herself. Hoku shouldn't feel tension quaking off her.

After three quiet breaths, Darby leaned her shoulder against Hoku's.

The filly didn't shift away. Instead, she rearranged her front hooves to return the gentle pressure.

"Perfect," Darby barely breathed the word before raising her arms in a hug and rubbing the filly's poll.

At last Hoku relaxed. Her head drooped until her lips were even with Darby's knees.

Now came the hard part. Could she tie a soft rope halter on Hoku's lowered head?

"Stay close," Cade repeated.

Darby guessed she should have given some sign that she'd heard him the first time, but Cade had studied the way of Hawaii's cowboys, the paniolo, and he was apprenticed to her grandfather Jonah, a man known as the Hawaiian horse charmer. Shouldn't a horseman like Cade know she didn't want to set off Hoku?

"Hear me?" Cade asked.

Darby risked a tiny nod. That was all it took to detonate the filly's wildness.

Hoku bolted into a gallop. Strides meant to cross an endless range took her around and around the corral.

Darby kept herself from groaning, but her arm had a mind of its own. It flung the orange rope halter down in frustration.

Hoku's front legs lifted. Her hooves jounced down as if she'd pound the life out of a snake Darby had thrown in her path. Then, Hoku wheeled and raced in the opposite direction.

"Temper just set you back an hour," Cade pointed out, but she still didn't look at him.

She knew what she'd see: brown eyes set in a sun-browned face beneath a brown luahala hat that hid the only spot of color about him, the tight blond braid of a paniolo.

Squinting her eyes against the dust swirling around her, Darby snatched up the halter. She sorted it back into shape by touch, without taking her eyes off the horse.

Reversing her morning's progress, Darby backed

toward the fence until she collided with it.

"Go away. Please."

"Jonah wants me to supervise—"

"But—"

"And he's the boss," Cade finished.

Wishing she could communicate with Cade as well as she could with Hoku, Darby considered the hand-me-down boots she'd accepted from Megan Kato, the ranch manager's daughter. Scuffed through the reddish finish of the oxblood leather, they were real cowgirl boots and Darby loved them, but they didn't supply any ideas on how to convince Cade she needed to be alone with her horse.

"We'll be okay," Darby promised, and when Cade didn't contradict her, she slid her eyes around far enough to see he was staring up at the pillowy gray clouds.

"Suppose it's this storm that's got Luna so spooky?" Cade asked her, and Darby heard the stallion neighing from the lower pastures again, though he was usually quiet during the day.

"It doesn't look like much," Darby said. Though she hadn't been in Hawaii long, the clouds didn't look like they were holding a downpour that would send her scurrying inside to curl up on her bed and read. "Maybe you should go check on him."

This second silence had to mean a weakening in Cade's resolve.

"Maybe I will," Cade said. "Something's got him stirred up." He pushed back from the fence so abruptly, the post joint creaked with a sound like a starter's gun. "Be right back."

Yes! Cade's retreat worked like magic. As he turned his back, Hoku slowed to a jog, then a walk. Then, she stopped, sneezing at the dust halo she'd raised.

"Hoku," Darby greeted as if she hadn't seen her horse for days, and the filly watched Darby tighten her black ponytail. "Here's what I think. We need to stop worrying about what Shan Stonerow did to you and get on with our lives."

When the sorrel sidestepped, Darby decided that wasn't a concept a horse could grasp.

"I know," Darby sympathized, "he was a bad guy. He hit you in the face, but that won't happen ever again."

Darby closed her eyes, trying to send the filly an image of snow melting off the range, of warmth replacing cold.

"We're starting over, like springtime."